Abraham Lincoln

Early speeches

Springfield speech, Cooper union speech, inaugural addresses, Gettysburg address,

selected letters, Lincoln's lost speech - Vol. 1

Abraham Lincoln

Early speeches
Springfield speech, Cooper union speech, inaugural addresses, Gettysburg address, selected letters, Lincoln's lost speech - Vol. 1

ISBN/EAN: 9783337377618

Printed in Europe, USA, Canada, Australia, Japan

Cover: Foto ©Andreas Hilbeck / pixelio.de

More available books at **www.hansebooks.com**

Little Masterpieces

Edited by Bliss Perry

ABRAHAM LINCOLN

EARLY SPEECHES

SPRINGFIELD SPEECH

COOPER UNION SPEECH

INAUGURAL ADDRESSES

GETTYSBURG ADDRESS

SELECTED LETTERS

LINCOLN'S LOST SPEECH

NEW YORK

DOUBLEDAY & McCLURE CO.

1898

" He knew to bide his time,
    And can his fame abide,
    Still patient in his simple faith sublime,
    Till the wise years decide.
    Great captains, with their guns and drums,
    Disturb our judgment for the hour,
    But at last silence comes ;
    These all are gone, and, standing like a
        tower,
    Our children shall behold his fame,
    The kindly-earnest, brave, foreseeing man.
    Sagacious, patient, dreading praise, not
        blame,
    New birth of our new soil, the first Ameri-
        can."
                LOWELL, *Commemoration Ode.*

Introduction

▼

Editor's Introduction

" It is not too much to say of him [Lincoln] that he is among the greatest masters of prose ever produced by the English race."—*The (London) Spectator.*

It is said that Nathaniel Hawthorne was once asked the secret of his style. That consummate writer replied—no doubt with one of his inscrutable smiles—" It is the result of a great deal of practice. It comes from the desire to tell the simple truth as honestly and vividly as I can." The flawless perfection of Lincoln's style in his noblest utterances eludes a final analysis as completely as the exquisite pages of our great romancer, yet in striving to understand some of the causes of that perfection we may use the hint which Hawthorne has given us

Lincoln had " a great deal of practice" in the art of speech long before his debates against Douglas made him known to the nation : endless talks in country stores, endless jests in frontier taverns, twenty years of pleading in the circuit courts, twenty-five years of constant political discussion. His law partner has noted his incessant interest in the precise meaning of words. His reputation for clear statement to

Introduction

a jury was the result of his passion for putting ideas into language " plain enough for any boy to comprehend." Lincoln's mind worked slowly, and he was long in finding the words that exactly expressed his thoughts, but when he had once hit upon the word or phrase he never forgot it. " He read less and thought more than any man in the country," says Herndon with a sort of pride, and it should be remembered that throughout his gradual development as a master of his mother tongue he was preoccupied, not with words for their own sake, but solely with words as the garb of ideas.

Furthermore, Lincoln's mental characteristics illustrate with singular force the remark of Hawthorne that style is the result of a desire to tell the simple truth as honestly and vividly as one can. He was " Honest Abe ;" not indeed so innocent and frank and unsophisticated as many people believed ; not a man who told all he knew, by any means ; but yet a man essentially fair-minded. He looked into the nature of things. He read human nature dispassionately. A man of intense feeling, he was never theless, in mature life at least, without sentimentality. He was not fooled by phrases. As a debater, he made no attempt to mislead his audience ; as President, when he found frank conversation impossible, he told a humorous story of more or less remote bearing upon the subject in hand. He kept inviolate his mental integrity. And without integrity of mind the

Introduction

would-be master of speech becomes a mere jug-
gler with words. In the letter to Thurlow
Weed concerning the Second Inaugural Address, Lincoln described that memorable utter-
ance as " a truth which I thought needed to be
told." No description could be more noble.

That Lincoln's gift of humor added much to
the vividness and homely naturalness of his
style will not be questioned. But the connection between fair-mindedness and humor is not
always remembered. The man of true humor
—not, of course, the mere joker or wit—sees all
sides of a proposition. He recognizes instinc-
tively its defects of proportion, its incongruities.
It is the great humorists who have drawn the
truest pictures of human life, because their
humor was a constant corrective against one-
sidedness. Lincoln's mind had the impartial-
ity, the freedom from prejudice, the flexibility
of sympathy, which belongs to the humorist
alone.

It has sometimes been argued that his fond-
ness for story-telling showed a deficient command of language ; that knowing his inability
to express his ideas directly, he conveyed them
indirectly by an anecdote. It would probably
be nearer the truth to say that the stories were
a proof of his understanding of the limitations
of language. He divined the boundaries of expression through formal speech, and knew
when a picture, a parable, would best serve his
turn.

Introduction

As great responsibilities came to rest upon him, as the harassing problems of our national life pressed closer and closer, the lonely President grew more clear-eyed and certain of his course. The politician was lost in the states- man. His whole life, indeed, was a process of enfranchisement from selfish and narrow views. He stood at last on a serener height than other men of his epoch, breathing an ampler air, per- ceiving more truly the eternal realities. And his style changed as the man changed. What he saw and felt at his solitary final post he has in part made known, through a slowly perfected instrument of expression. So transparent is the language of the Gettysburg Address and of the Second Inaugural that one may read through them, as through a window, Lincoln's wise and gentle and unselfish heart. Other praise is needless.

The selections included in this volume are designed to illustrate the steady development of Lincoln's literary power. They begin with a few specimens of his earlier style, which was direct, forceful, and manly, but not markedly better than that of many of his contemporaries. The famous " Lost Speech" of May 29, 1856, has been reprinted in the Appendix. As it does not present Lincoln's exact language throughout, it could scarcely be placed with the other selections, but its personal and historical interest is so great that lovers of Lincoln will be glad to have it preserved in convenient form.

Introduction

With the Springfield speech of June 16, 1858, Lincoln entered upon a new phase of his career. His careful enunciation of a great political principle made it the turning-point of a memorable campaign. The significance of its opening paragraph, in particular, has been discussed in the prefatory note to the speech itself, and need not be repeated here. The space-limit of the volumes in this series forbids the presentation of any of the entire speeches of the joint debates with Douglas, and so closely inter-related, so full of allusion and cross reference are all of those speeches that detached paragraphs would give little conception of the qualities displayed by either of the debaters. The Cooper Union speech of February 25, 1860, however, goes over much of the ground of the Douglas debates.

The remaining speeches in the volume belong to Lincoln's career as President. They range from the most informal addresses to the Inaugurals. The Emancipation Proclamation is also included. The letters exhibit still another side of Lincoln's strange and fascinating individuality. In compression and clear-cut force, in their humor and homely pathos, in their shrewd knowledge of character, these letters are among the most extraordinary ever written. While they afford new glimpses into Lincoln's nature, it is true of them, as it is of his other writings, that they express without explaining the secret of his personality. One closes a vol-

Introduction

ume of Lincoln's addresses and letters with
something of the feeling that Walt Whitman
has uttered with regard to Lincoln's portraits :
" None of the artists or pictures has caught the
deep though subtle and indirect expression of
this man's face. *There is something else
there.*"

BLISS PERRY.

CONTENTS

PAGE

Editor's Introduction . . . v

Speeches—Selected

The Whigs and the Mexican War . 3
Notes for a Law Lecture . . 7
Fragment on Slavery . . . 11
The Dred Scott Decision and the
  Declaration of Independence . 13
Springfield Speech . . . 23
Cooper Union Speech . . . 37
Farewell at Springfield . . 70
Speech in Independence Hall, Phila-
  delphia 71
First Inaugural Address . . 74
Emancipation Proclamation . . 90
Gettysburg Address . . . 94
Speech to 166th Ohio Regiment . 96
Response to a Serenade . . 98
Reply to Committee on Electoral Count 101
Second Inaugural Address . . 102

Letters

To McClellan 109
To Seward 111
To Greeley 113
To the Workingmen of Manchester . 115
To Hooker 118
To Burnside 120
To Edward Everett . . . 121
To Grant 122
To Mrs. Bixby 123
To Thurlow Weed . . . 124

Appendix

Lincoln's Lost Speech . . . 127

Selected Speeches

Selections from Lincoln's Speeches and Letters

The Whigs and the Mexican War

July 27, 1848

[An extract from a speech delivered in the House of Representatives while Lincoln was a Congressman from Illinois. The speech was in support of General Taylor, the Whig candidate for the Presidency. Lincoln had opposed President Polk's declaration of war against Mexico, had introduced resolutions of inquiry on that subject, and made a strong speech on January 12, 1848, explaining his own attitude. The speech of July 27 was full of wit, at times more caustic than refined. The extract here presented sums up clearly Lincoln's views as to the Mexican War, and is a good example of his best parliamentary style at this stage of his career.]

BUT, as General Taylor is, *par excellence*, the hero of the Mexican War, and as you Democrats say we Whigs have always opposed the war, you think it must be very awkward and embarrassing for us to go for General Taylor. The declaration that we have always opposed the war is true or false, according as one may understand the term " oppose the war." If to say " the war was unnecessarily and unconsti-

Abraham Lincoln

tutionally commenced by the President" be opposing the war, then the Whigs have very generally opposed it.   Whenever they have spoken
at all, they have said this ; and they have said
it on what has appeared good reason to them.
The marching an army into the midst of a
peaceful Mexican settlement, frightening the
inhabitants away, leaving their growing crops
and other property to destruction, to you may
appear a perfectly amiable, peaceful, unprovok-
ing procedure ; but it does not appear so to us.
So to call such an act, to us appears no other
than a naked, impudent absurdity, and we
speak of it accordingly.   But if, when the war
had begun, and had become the cause of the
country, the giving of our money and our blood,
in common with yours, was support of the war,
then it is not true that we have always opposed
the war.   With few individual exceptions, you
have constantly had our votes here for all the
necessary supplies.   And, more than this, you
have had the services, the blood, and the lives
of our political brethren in every trial and on
every field.   The beardless boy and the mature
man, the humble and the distinguished—you
have had them.   Through suffering and death,
by disease and in battle, they have endured and
fought and fell with you.   Clay and Webster
each gave a son, never to be returned.   From
the State of my own residence, besides other
worthy but less known Whig names, we sent
Marshall, Morrison, Baker, and Hardin ; they

4

all fought, and one fell, and in the fall of that one we lost our best Whig man. Nor were the Whigs few in number, or laggard in the day of danger. In that fearful, bloody, breathless struggle at Buena Vista, where each man's hard task was to beat back five foes or die himself, of the five high officers who perished, four were Whigs.

In speaking of this, I mean no odious comparison between the lion-hearted Whigs and the Democrats who fought there. On other occasions, and among the lower officers and privates on that occasion, I doubt not the proportion was different. I wish to do justice to all. I think of all those brave men as Americans, in whose proud fame, as an American, I too have a share. Many of them, Whigs and Democrats, are my constituents and personal friends ; and I thank them,—more than thank them,—one and all, for the high imperishable honor they have conferred on our common State.

But the distinction between the cause of the President in beginning the war, and the cause of the country after it was begun, is a distinction which you cannot perceive. To you the President and the country seem to be all one. You are interested to see no distinction between them ; and I venture to suggest that probably your interest blinds you a little. We see the distinction, as we think, clearly enough ; and our friends who have fought in the war have no difficulty in seeing it also. What those who have fallen would say, were they alive and here, of course we can never know ; but with those who have returned there is no difficulty. Colonel Haskell and Major Gaines, members here, both fought in the war, and one of them underwent extraordinary perils and hardships ; still they, like all other Whigs here, vote, on the record, that the war was unnecessarily and unconstitutionally commenced by the President. And even General Taylor himself, the noblest Roman of them all, has declared that as a citizen, and particularly as a soldier, it is sufficient for him to know that his country is at war with a foreign nation, to do all in his power to bring it to a speedy and honorable termination by the most vigorous and energetic operations, without inquiry about its justice, or anything else connected with it.

Mr. Speaker. let our Democratic friends be comforted with the assurance that we are content with our position, content with our company, and content with our candidate ; and that although they, in their generous sympathy, think we ought to be miserable, we really are not, and that they may dismiss the great anxiety they have on our account.

Notes for a Law Lecture

July 1, 1850

[These notes show Lincoln's power of straight-forward statement and his good sense. They are of additional interest as indicating his attitude toward professional success.]

I AM not an accomplished lawyer. I find quite as much material for a lecture in those points wherein I have failed as in those wherein I have been moderately successful. The leading rule for the lawyer, as for the man of every other calling, is diligence. Leave nothing for to-morrow which can be done to-day. Never let your correspondence fall behind. Whatever piece of business you have in hand, before stopping, do all the labor pertaining to it which can then be done. When you bring a common-law suit, if you have the facts for doing so, write the declaration at once. If a law point be involved, examine the books, and note the authority you rely on upon the declaration itself, where you are sure to find it when wanted. The same of defenses and pleas. In business not likely to be litigated,—ordinary collection cases, foreclosures, partitions, and the like,—

7

make all examinations of titles, and note them, and even draft orders and decrees in advance. This course has a triple advantage ; it avoids omissions and neglect, saves your labor when once done, performs the labor out of court when you have leisure, rather than in court when you have not. Extemporaneous speaking should be practised and cultivated. It is the lawyer's avenue to the public. However able and faithful he may be in other respects, people are slow to bring him business if he cannot make a speech. And yet there is not a more fatal error to young lawyers than relying too much on speech-making. If any one, upon his rare powers of speaking, shall claim an exemption from the drudgery of the law, his case is a failure in advance.

Discourage litigation. Persuade your neighbors to compromise whenever you can. Point out to them how the nominal winner is often a real loser—in fees, expenses, and waste of time. As a peacemaker the lawyer has a superior opportunity of being a good man. There will still be business enough.

Never stir up litigation. A worse man can scarcely be found than one who does this. Who can be more nearly a fiend than he who habitually overhauls the register of deeds in search of defects in titles, whereon to stir up strife, and put money in his pocket? A moral tone ought to be infused into the profession which should drive such men out of it.

Notes for a Law Lecture

The matter of fees is important, far beyond the mere question of bread and butter involved. Properly attended to, fuller justice is done to both lawyer and client. An exorbitant fee should never be claimed. As a general rule never take your whole fee in advance, nor any more than a small retainer. When fully paid beforehand, you are more than a common mortal if you can feel the same interest in the case, as if something was still in prospect for you, as well as for your client. And when you lack interest in the case the job will very likely lack skill and diligence in the performance. Settle the amount of fee and take a note in advance. Then you will feel that you are working for something, and you are sure to do your work faithfully and well. Never sell a fee note—at least not before the consideration service is performed. It leads to negligence and dishonesty —negligence by losing interest in the case, and dishonesty in refusing to refund when you have allowed the consideration to fail.

There is a vague popular belief that lawyers are necessarily dishonest. I say vague, because when we consider to what extent confidence and honors are reposed in and conferred upon lawyers by the people, it appears improbable that their impression of dishonesty is very distinct and vivid. Yet the impression is common, almost universal. Let no young man choosing the law for a calling for a moment yield to the popular belief—resolve to be honest at all

events ; and if in your own judgment you cannot be an honest lawyer, resolve to be honest
without being a lawyer. Choose some other
occupation, rather than one in the choosing of
which you do, in advance, consent to be a
knave.

Fragment on Slavery

July 1, 1854

[From early manhood Lincoln's sympathies had been strongly enlisted on behalf of the slaves. The contrast between slave labor and free labor has never been stated more tersely and vividly than here. The sentence, "Twenty-five years ago I was a hired laborer," should be noted.]

EQUALITY in society alike beats inequality, whether the latter be of the British aristocratic sort or of the domestic slavery sort. We know Southern men declare that their slaves are better off than hired laborers amongst us. How little they know whereof they speak ! There is no permanent class of hired laborers amongst us. Twenty-five years ago I was a hired laborer. The hired laborer of yesterday labors on his own account to-day, and will hire others to labor for him to-morrow. Advancement—improvement in condition—is the order of things in a society of equals. As labor is the common burden of our race, so the effort of some to shift their share of the burden onto the shoulders of others is the great durable curse of the race.

Abraham Lincoln

Originally a curse for transgression upon the whole race, when, as by slavery, it is concentrated on a part only, it becomes the double-refined curse of God upon his creatures.

Free labor has the inspiration of hope ; pure slavery has no hope. The power of hope upon human exertion and happiness is wonderful. The slave-master himself has a conception of it, and hence the system of tasks among slaves. The slave whom you cannot drive with the lash to break seventy-five pounds of hemp in a day, if you will task him to break a hundred, and promise him pay for all he does over, he will break you a hundred and fifty. You have substituted hope for the rod. And yet perhaps it does not occur to you that to the extent of your gain in the case, you have given up the slave system and adopted the free system of labor.

The Dred Scott Decision and the Declaration of Independence

June 26, 1857

[This is an extract from a speech delivered in Springfield, Ill. It was intended as a reply to a speech of Stephen A. Douglas two weeks earlier upon the subject of slavery in the Territories. Douglas was the author of the Kansas-Nebraska bill, passed in 1854, which gave the Territories the right to decide whether they would have slavery. The Dred Scott decision was published by the Supreme Court of the United States in 1857, and was ˌ the effect that a slave or the descendant of ˌ slave could not be a citizen of the United States or have any standing in the Federal courts. Lincoln contrasts the spirit of this decision with that of the Declaration of Independence, with a skill and force that will be apparent to every reader. He repeated the substance of the argument over and over again in his joint debates with Douglas in the following year.]

I HAVE said, in substance, that the Dred Scott decision was in part based on assumed historical facts which were not really true, and I ought not to leave the subject without giving some reasons for saying this ; I therefore give an instance or two, which I think fully sustain me. Chief Justice Taney, in delivering the opinion of the majority of the court, insists at great length that negroes were no part of the people who made, or for whom was made, the Declaration of Independence, or the Constitution of the United States.

On the contrary, Judge Curtis, in his dissenting opinion, shows that in five of the then thirteen States—to wit, New Hampshire, Massachusetts, New York, New Jersey, and North Carolina—free negroes were voters, and in proportion to their numbers had the same part in making the Constitution that the white people had.   He shows this with so much particularity as to leave no doubt of its truth ; and as a sort of conlusion on that point, holds the following language :

" The Constitution was ordained and established by the people of the United States, through the action, in each State, of those persons who were qualified by its laws to act thereon in behalf of themselves and all other citizens of the State.   In some of the States, as we have seen, colored persons were among those qualified by law to act on the subject.   These colored persons were not only included in the body of ' the people of the United States ' by whom the Constitution was ordained and established ; but in at least five of the States they had the power to act, and doubtless did act, by their suffrages, upon the question of its adoption."

Again, Chief Justice Taney says :

" It is difficult at this day to realize the state of public opinion, in relation to that unfortunate race, which prevailed in the civilized and enlightened portions of the world at the time of the Declaration of Independence, and when the Constitution of the United States was framed and adopted."

And again, after quoting from the Declaration, he says :

"The general words above quoted would seem to include the whole human family, and if they were used in a similar instrument at this day, would be so understood."

In these the Chief Justice does not directly assert but plainly assumes, as a fact, that the public estimate of the black man is more favorable now than it was in the days of the Revolution. This assumption is a mistake. In some trifling particulars the condition of that race has been ameliorated ; but as a whole, in this country, the change between then and now is decidedly the other way ; and their ultimate destiny has never appeared so hopeless as in the last three or four years. In two of the five States—New Jersey and North Carolina—that then gave the free negro the right of voting, the right has since been taken away, and in a third—New York—it has been greatly abridged ; while it has not been extended, so far as I know, to a single additional State, though the number of the States has more than doubled. In those days, as I understand, masters could, at their own pleasure, emancipate their slaves ; but since then such legal restraints have been made upon emancipation as to amount almost to prohibition. In those days legislatures held the unquestioned power to abolish slavery in their respective States, but now it is becoming quite fashionable for State constitutions to withhold that power from the legislatures. In those days, by common consent, the spread of the black man's bondage to the new countries was prohibited, but now Congress decides that it will not continue the prohibition, and the Supreme Court decides that it could not if it would. In those days our Declaration of Independence was held sacred by all, and thought to include all ; but now, to aid in making the bondage of the negro universal and eternal, it is assailed and sneered at and construed, and hawked at and torn, till, if its framers could rise from their graves, they could not at all recognize it. All the powers of earth seem rapidly combining against him. Mammon is after him, ambition follows, philosophy follows, and the theology of the day is fast joining the cry. They have him in his prison-house ; they have searched his person, and left no prying instrument with him. One after another they have closed the heavy iron doors upon him ; and now they have him, as it were, bolted in with a lock of a hundred keys, which can never be unlocked without the concurrence of every key—the keys in the hands of a hundred different men, and they scattered to a hundred different and distant places ; and they stand musing as to what invention, in all the dominions of mind and matter, can be produced to make the impossibility of his escape more complete than it is.

It is grossly incorrect to say or assume that the public estimate of the negro is more favorable now than it was at the origin of the government.

Three years and a half ago, Judge Douglas brought forward his famous Nebraska bill. The country was at once in a blaze. He scorned all opposition, and carried it through Congress. Since then he has seen himself superseded in a presidential nomination by one indorsing the general doctrine of his measure, but at the same time standing clear of the odium of its untimely agitation and its gross breach of national faith ; and he has seen that successful rival constitutionally elected, not by the strength of friends, but by the division of adversaries, being in a popular minority of nearly four hundred thousand votes. He has seen his chief aids in his own State, Shields and Richardson, politically speaking, successively tried, convicted, and executed for an offense not their own, but his. And now he sees his own case standing next on the docket for trial.

There is a natural disgust in the minds of nearly all white people at the idea of an indiscriminate amalgamation of the white and black races ; and Judge Douglas evidently is basing his chief hope upon the chances of his being able to appropriate the benefit of this disgust to himself. If he can, by much drumming and repeating, fasten the odium of that idea upon his adversaries, he thinks he can struggle through the storm. He therefore clings to this hope, as a drowning man to the last plank. He makes an occasion for lugging it in from the opposition to the Dred Scott decision. He finds the Republicans insisting that the Declaration of Independence includes *all* men, black as well as white, and forthwith he boldly denies that it includes negroes at all, and proceeds to argue gravely that all who contend it does, do so only because they want to vote, and eat, and sleep, and marry with negroes ! He will have it that they cannot be consistent else. Now I protest against the counterfeit logic which concludes that, because I do not want a black woman for a slave I must necessarily want her for a wife. I need not have her for either. I can just leave her alone. In some respects she certainly is not my equal ; but in her natural right to eat the bread she earns with her own hands without asking leave of any one else, she is my equal, and the equal of all others.

Chief Justice Taney, in his opinion in the Dred Scott case, admits that the language of the Declaration is broad enough to include the whole human family, but he and Judge Douglas argue that the authors of that instrument did not intend to include negroes, by the fact that they did not at once actually place them on an equality with the whites. Now this grave argument comes to just nothing at all, by the other

fact that they did not at once, or ever afterward, actually place all white people on an
equality with one another. And this is the
staple argument of both the chief justice and
the senator for doing this obvious violence to
the plain, unmistakable language of the Declaration.

I think the authors of that notable instrument
intended to include *all* men, but they did not
intend to declare all men equal *in all respects*.
They did not mean to say all were equal in
color, size, intellect, moral developments, or
social capacity. They defined with tolerable
distinctness in what respects they did consider
all men created equal—equal with " certain inalienable rights, among which are life, liberty,
and the pursuit of happiness." This they said,
and this they meant. They did not mean to
assert the obvious untruth that all were then
actually enjoying that equality, nor yet that
they were about to confer it immediately upon
them. In fact, they had no power to confer
such a boon. They meant simply to declare
the right, so that enforcement of it might follow as fast as circumstances should permit.

They meant to set up a standard maxim for
free society, which should be familiar to all,
and revered by all ; constantly looked to, constantly labored for, and even though never perfectly attained, constantly approximated, and
thereby constantly spreading and deepening its
influence and augmenting the happiness and

value of life to all people of all colors everywhere. The assertion that " all men are created equal" was of no practical use in effecting
our separation from Great Britain ; and it was
placed in the Declaration not for that, but for
future use. Its authors meant it to be—as,
thank God, it is now proving itself—a stum-
bling-block to all those who in after-times might
seek to turn a free people back into the hateful
paths of despotism. They knew the proneness
of prosperity to breed tyrants, and they meant
when such should reappear in this fair land and
commence their vocation, they should find left
for them at least one hard nut to crack.

I have now briefly expressed my view of the
meaning and object of that part of the Declaration of Independence which declares that " all
men are created equal."

Now let us hear Judge Douglas's view of the
same subject, as I find it in the printed report
of his late speech. Here it is :

" No man can vindicate the character, motives, and conduct of the signers of the Declaration of Independence, except upon the hypoth-
esis that they referred to the white race alone,
and not to the African, when they declared all
men to have been created equal ; that they
were speaking of British subjects on this continent being equal to British subjects born and
residing in Great Britain ; that they were entitled to the same inalienable rights, and among
them were enumerated life, liberty, and the
pursuit of happiness. The Declaration was
adopted for the purpose of justifying the colo-

nists in the eyes of the civilized world in with-
drawing their allegiance from the British crown,
and dissolving their connection with the mother
country."

My good friends, read that carefully over
some leisure hour, and ponder well upon it ;
see what a mere wreck —mangled ruin—it
makes of our once glorious Declaration.

" They were speaking of British subjects on
this continent being equal to British subjects
born and residing in Great Britain !" Why,
according to this, not only negroes but white
people outside of Great Britain and America
were not spoken of in that instrument. The
English, Irish, and Scotch, along with white
Americans, were included, to be sure, but the
French, Germans, and other white people of
the world are all gone to pot along with the
judge's inferior races !

I had thought the Declaration promised something better than the condition of British subjects ; but no, it only meant that we should be
equal to them in their own oppressed and un-
equal condition. According to that, it gave no
promise that, having kicked off the king and
lords of Great Britain, we should not at once
be saddled with a king and lords of our own.

I had thought the Declaration contemplated
the progressive improvement in the condition
of all men everywhere ; but no, it merely " was
adopted for the purpose of justifying the colo-
nists in the eyes of the civilized world in with-

drawing their allegiance from the British crown, and dissolving their connection with the mother country." Why, that object having been effected some eighty years ago, the Declaration is of no practical use now—mere rubbish—old wadding left to rot on the battle-field after the victory is won.

I understand you are preparing to celebrate the "Fourth," to-morrow week. What for? The doings of that day had no reference to the present; and quite half of you are not even descendants of those who were referred to at that day. But I suppose you will celebrate, and will even go so far as to read the Declaration. Suppose, after you read it once in the old-fashioned way, you read it once more with Judge Douglas's version. It will then run thus: " We hold these truths to be self-evident, that all British subjects who were on this continent eighty-one years ago, were created equal to all British subjects born and then residing in Great Britain."

And now I appeal to ail—to Democrats as well as others—are you really willing that the Declaration shall thus be frittered away?—thus left no more, at most, than an interesting memorial of the dead past?—thus shorn of its vitality and practical value, and left without the germ or even the suggestion of the individual rights of man in it?

Springfield Speech

June 16, 1858

Speech delivered at Springfield, Illinois, at the
close of the Republican State Convention by
which Mr. Lincoln had been named as their
candidate for United States Senator.

[The opening paragraph of this speech was
prepared with the most extreme care, and probably did more to influence Lincoln's political
future than anything he ever wrote. His best
friends thought it impolitic to utter the sentiment that the " government cannot endure permanently half slave and half free."
For the immediate purpose of that campaign
they were right, for this paragraph, in the opinion of many good judges, was the cause of Lincoln's defeat by Douglas. But the constant
discussion of those sentences in the great series
of joint debates with Douglas during the summer and autumn brought Lincoln's views before the whole country, and was an important
element in his selection as the Republican candidate for the Presidency in 1860. The entire
speech, read in the light of subsequent history,
affords remarkable evidence not only of Lincoln's shrewdness as a party leader, but of his
political wisdom in the highest sense.]

*Mr. President and Gentlemen of the Con-
vention :* If we could first know where we are,
and whither we are tending, we could better

judge what to do, and how to do it. We are now far into the fifth year since a policy was initiated with the avowed object and confident promise of putting an end to slavery agitation. Under the operation of that policy, that agitation has not only not ceased, but has constantly augmented. In my opinion, it will not cease until a crisis shall have been. reached and passed. "A house divided against itself cannot stand." I believe this government cannot endure permanently half slave and half free. I do not expect the Union to be dissolved—I do not expect the house to fall —but I do expect it will cease to be divided. It will become all one thing, or all the other. Either the opponents of slavery will arrest the further spread of it, and place it where the public mind shall rest in the belief that it is in the course of ultimate extinction ; or its advocates will push it forward till it shall become alike lawful in all the States, old as well as new, North as well as South.

Have we no tendency to the latter condition ?

Let any one who doubts carefully contemplate that now almost complete legal combination—piece of machinery, so to speak—compounded of the Nebraska doctrine and the Dred Scott decision. Let him consider not only what work the machinery is adapted to do, and how well adapted ; but also let him study the history of its construction, and trace, if he can, or rather fail, if he can, to trace the evidences of design and concert of action among its chief architects, from the beginning.

The new year of 1854 found slavery excluded from more than half the States by State constitutions, and from most of the national territory by congressional prohibition. Four days later commenced the struggle which ended in repealing that congressional prohibition. This opened all the national territory to slavery, and was the first point gained.

But, so far, Congress only had acted ; and an indorsement by the people, real or apparent, was indispensable to save the point already gained and give chance for more.

This necessity had not been overlooked, but had been provided for, as well as might be, in the notable argument of "squatter sovereignty," otherwise called "sacred right of self-government," which latter phrase, though expressive of the only rightful basis of any government, was so perverted in this attempted use of it as to amount to just this : That if any one man choose to enslave another, no third man shall be allowed to object. That argument was incorporated into the Nebraska bill itself, in the language which follows : "It being the true intent and meaning of this act not to legislate slavery into any Territory or State, nor to exclude it therefrom ; but to leave the people thereof perfectly free to form and regulate their domestic institutions in their own way, subject only to the Constitution of the United States."

Then opened the roar of loose declamation in favor of "squatter sovereignty" and "sacred right of self-government." "But," said opposition members, "let us amend the bill so as to expressly declare that the people of the Territory may exclude slavery." "Not we," said the friends of the measure; and down they voted the amendment.

While the Nebraska bill was passing through Congress, a law case involving the question of a negro's freedom, by reason of his owner having voluntarily taken him first into a free State and then into a Territory covered by the congressional prohibition, and held him as a slave for a long time in each, was passing through the United States Circuit Court for the District of Missouri; and both Nebraska bill and lawsuit were brought to a decision in the same month of May, 1854. The negro's name was Dred Scott, which name now designates the decision finally made in the case. Before the then next presidential election, the law case came to and was argued in the Supreme Court of the United States; but the decision of it was deferred until after the election. Still, before the election, Senator Trumbull, on the floor of the Senate, requested the leading advocate of the Nebraska bill to state his opinion whether the people of a Territory can constitutionally exclude slavery from their limits; and the latter answered: "That is a question for the Supreme Court."

Springfield Speech

The election came. Mr. Buchanan was elected, and the indorsement, such as it was, secured. That was the second point gained. The indorsement, however, fell short of a clear popular majority by nearly four hundred thousand votes, and so, perhaps, was not overwhelmingly reliable and satisfactory. The outgoing President, in his last annual message, as impressively as possible echoed back upon the people the weight and authority of the indorsement. The Supreme Court met again ; did not announce their decision, but ordered a reargument. The presidential inauguration came, and still no decision of the court ; but the incoming President in his inaugural address fervently exhorted the people to abide by the forthcoming decision, whatever it might be. Then, in a few days, came the decision.

The reputed author of the Nebraska bill finds an early occasion to make a speech at this capital indorsing the Dred Scott decision, and vehemently denouncing all opposition to it. The new President, too, seizes the early occasion of the Silliman letter to indorse and strongly construe that decision, and to express his astonishment that any different view had ever been entertained !

At length a squabble springs up between the President and the author of the Nebraska bill, on the mere question of fact, whether the Lecompton constitution was or was not, in any just sense, made by the people of Kansas ; and

Abraham Lincoln

in that quarrel the latter declares that all he
wants is a fair vote for the people, and that he
cares not whether slavery be voted down or
voted up. I do not understand his declaration
that he cares not whether slavery be voted
down or voted up to be intended by him other
than as an apt definition of the policy he would
impress upon the public mind—the principle
for which he declares he has suffered so much,
and is ready to suffer to the end. And well
may he cling to that principle. If he has any
parental feeling, well may he cling to it. That
principle is the only shred left of his original
Nebraska doctrine. Under the Dred Scott decision "squatter sovereignty" squatted out of
existence, tumbled down like temporary scaffolding,—like the mold at the foundry, served
through one blast and fell back into loose sand,
—helped to carry an election, and then was
kicked to the winds. His late joint struggle
with the Republicans against the Lecompton
constitution involves nothing of the original
Nebraska doctrine. That struggle was made
on a point—the right of a people to make their
own constitution—upon which he and the Republicans have never differed.

The several points of the Dred Scott decision,
in connection with Senator Douglas's "care
not" policy, constitute the piece of machinery
in its present state of advancement. This was
the third point gained. The working points of
that machinery are :

Springfield Speech

(1) That no negro slave, imported as such from Africa, and no descendant of such slave, can ever be a citizen of any State, in the sense of that term as used in the Constitution of the United States. This point is made in order to deprive the negro in every possible event of the benefit of that provision of the United States Constitution which declares that "the citizens of each State shall be entitled to all the privileges and immunities of citizens in the several States."

(2) That, "subject to the Constitution of the United States," neither Congress nor a territorial legislature can exclude slavery from any United States Territory. This point is made in order that individual men may fill up the Territories with slaves, without danger of losing them as property, and thus enhance the chances of permanency to the institution through all the future.

(3) That whether the holding a negro in actual slavery in a free State makes him free as against the holder, the United States courts will not decide, but will leave to be decided by the courts of any slave State the negro may be forced into by the master. This point is made not to be pressed immediately, but, if acquiesced in for a while and apparently indorsed by the people at an election, then to sustain the logical conclusion that what Dred Scott's master might lawfully do with Dred Scott in the free State of Illinois, every other master may law-

fully do with any other one or one thousand slaves in Illinois or in any other free State.

Auxiliary to all this, and working hand in hand with it, the Nebraska doctrine, or what is left of it, is to educate and mold public opinion, at least Northern public opinion, not to care whether slavery is voted down or voted up. This shows exactly where we now are, and partially, also, whither we are tending.

It will throw additional light on the latter, to go back and run the mind over the string of historical facts already stated. Several things will now appear less dark and mysterious than they did when they were transpiring. The people were to be left " perfectly free," " subject only to the Constitution." What the Constitution had to do with it outsiders could not then see. Plainly enough now, it was an exactly fitted niche for the Dred Scott decision to afterward come in, and declare the perfect freedom of the people to be just no freedom at all. Why was the amendment expressly declaring the right of the people voted down ? Plainly enough now, the adoption of it would have spoiled the niche for the Dred Scott decision. Why was the court decision held up ? Why even a senator's individual opinion withheld till after the presidential election ? Plainly enough now, the speaking out then would have damaged the " perfectly free" argument upon which the election was to be carried. Why the outgoing President's felicitation on the indorse-

ment? Why the delay of a reargument?
Why the incoming President's advance exhortation in favor of the decision? These things
look like the cautious patting and petting of a
spirited horse preparatory to mounting him,
when it is dreaded that he may give the rider a
fall. And why the hasty after-indorsement of
the decision by the President and others?

We cannot absolutely know that all these exact adaptations are the result of preconcert.
But when we see a lot of framed timbers, different portions of which we know have been gotten out at different times and places and by
different workmen,—Stephen, Franklin, Roger,
and James, for instance,—and we see these timbers joined together, and see they exactly make
the frame of a house or a mill, all the tenons
and mortises exactly fitting, and all the lengths
and proportions of the different pieces exactly
adapted to their respective places, and not a
piece too many or too few, not omitting even
scaffolding—or, if a single piece be lacking, we
see the place in the frame exactly fitted and
prepared yet to bring such piece in—in such a
case we find it impossible not to believe that
Stephen and Franklin and Roger and James all
understood one another from the beginning,
and all worked upon a common plan or draft
drawn up before the first blow was struck.

It should not be overlooked that, by the Nebraska bill, the people of a State as well as Territory were to be left " perfectly free," " subject only to the Constitution." Why mention a State? They were legislating for Territories, and not for or about States. Certainly the people of a State are and ought to be subject to the Constitution of the United States ; but why is mention of this lugged into this merely territorial law? Why are the people of a Territory and the people of a State therein lumped together, and their relation to the Constitution therein treated as being precisely the same? While the opinion of the court, by Chief Justice Taney, in the Dred Scott case, and the separate opinions of all the concurring judges, expressly declare that the Constitution of the United States neither permits Congress nor a territorial legislature to exclude slavery from any United States Territory, they all omit to declare whether or not the same Constitution permits a State, or the people of a State, to exclude it. Possibly, this is a mere omission ; but who can be quite sure, if McLean or Curtis had sought to get into the opinion a declaration of unlimited power in the people of a State to exclude slavery from their limits, just as Chase and Mace sought to get such declaration, in behalf of the people of a Territory, into the Nebraska bill—I ask, who can be quite sure that it would not have been voted down in the one case as it had been in the other? The nearest approach to the point of declaring the power of a State over slavery is made by Judge Nelson. He approaches it more than once, using the precise idea, and almost the language too, of the Nebraska act. On one occasion his exact language is: "Except in cases where the power is restrained by the Constitution of the United States, the law of the State is su-preme over the subject of slavery within its jurisdiction." In what cases the power of the States is so restrained by the United States Constitution is left an open question, precisely as the same question as to the restraint on the power of the Territories was left open in the Nebraska act. Put this and that together, and we have another nice little niche, which we may, ere long, see filled with another Supreme Court decision declaring that the Constitution of the United States does not permit a State to exclude slavery from its limits. And this may especially be expected if the doctrine of care not whether slavery be voted down or voted up" shall gain upon the public mind sufficiently to give promise that such a decision can be maintained when made.

Such a decision is all that slavery now lacks of being alike lawful in all the States. Welcome, or unwelcome, such decision is probably coming, and will soon be upon us, unless the power of the present political dynasty shall be met and overthrown. We shall lie down pleas-antly dreaming that the people of Missouri are on the verge of making their State free, and we shall awake to the reality instead that the Supreme Court has made Illinois a slave State.

To meet and overthrow the power of that dynasty is the work now before all those who would prevent that consummation. That is what we have to do. How can we best do it?

There are those who denounce us openly to their own friends, and yet whisper us softly that Senator Douglas is the aptest instrument there is with which to effect that object. They wish us to infer all from the fact that he now has a little quarrel with the present head of the dynasty ; and that he has regularly voted with us on a single point upon which he and we have never differed. They remind us that he is a great man, and that the largest of us are very small ones. Let this be granted. But "a living dog is better than a dead lion." Judge Douglas, if not a dead lion for this work, is at least a caged and toothless one. How can he oppose the advances of slavery? He don't care anything about it. His avowed mission is impressing the "public heart" to care nothing about it. A leading Douglas Democratic newspaper thinks Douglas's superior talent will be needed to resist the revival of the African slave-trade. Does Douglas believe an effort to revive that trade is approaching? He has not said so. Does he really think so? But if it is, how can he resist it? For years he has labored to prove it a sacred right of white men to take negro slaves into the new Territories. Can he possibly show that it is less a sacred right to buy them where they can be bought cheapest?

Springfield Speech

And unquestionably they can be bought cheaper in Africa than in Virginia. He has done all in his power to reduce the whole question of slavery to one of a mere right of property ; and as such, how can he oppose the foreign slave-trade? How can he refuse that trade in that "property" shall be "perfectly free," unless he does it as a protection to the home production ? And as the home producers will probably not ask the protection, he will be wholly without a ground of opposition.

Senator Douglas holds, we know, that a man may rightfully be wiser to-day than he was yesterday—that he may rightfully change when he finds himself wrong. But can we, for that reason, run ahead, and infer that he will make any particular change of which he, himself, has given no intimation ? Can we safely base our action upon any such vague inference ? Now, as ever, I wish not to misrepresent Judge Douglas's position, question his motives, or do aught that can be personally offensive to him. Whenever, if ever, he and we can come together on principle so that our great cause may have assistance from his great ability, I hope to have interposed no adventitious obstacle. But clearly, he is not now with us—he does not pretend to be—he does not promise ever to be.

Our cause, then, must be intrusted to, and conducted by, its own undoubted friends—those whose hands are free, whose hearts are in the work, who do care for the result. Two years

35

ago the Republicans of the nation mustered over thirteen hundred thousand strong. We did this under the single impulse of resistance to a common danger, with every external circumstance against us. Of strange, discordant, and even hostile elements, we gathered from the four winds, and formed and fought the battle through, under the constant hot fire of a disciplined, proud, and pampered enemy. Did we brave all then to falter now?—now, when that same enemy is wavering, dissevered, and belligerent? The result is not doubtful. We shall not fail—if we stand firm, we shall not fail. Wise counsels may accelerate or mistakes delay it, but, sooner or later, the victory is sure to come.

Address at Cooper Institute

February 27, 1860

[This was Lincoln's first appearance before an Eastern audience. The speech cost him a great deal of labor, and was most heartily received.—See *Morse's " Abraham Lincoln,"* I., 153–156.]

Mr. President and Fellow-citizens of New York: The facts with which I shall deal this evening are mainly old and familiar; nor is there anything new in the general use I shall make of them. If there shall be any novelty, it will be in the mode of presenting the facts, and the inferences and observations following that presentation. In his speech last autumn at Columbus, Ohio, as reported in the New York *Times*, Senator Douglas said :

" Our fathers, when they framed the government under which we live, understood this question just as well, and even better, than we do now."

I fully indorse this, and I adopt it as a text for this discourse. I so adopt it because it furnishes a precise and an agreed starting-point for a discussion between Republicans and that wing of the Democracy headed by Senator

Douglas. It simply leaves the inquiry : What was the understanding those fathers had of the question mentioned ?

What is the frame of government under which we live ? The answer must be, " The Constitution of the United States." That Constitution consists of the original, framed in 1787, and under which the present government first went into operation, and twelve subsequently framed amendments, the first ten of which were framed in 1789.

Who were our fathers that framed the Constitution ? I suppose the " thirty-nine" who signed the original instrument may be fairly called our fathers who framed that part of the present government. It is almost exactly true to say they framed it, and it is altogether true to say they fairly represented the opinion and sentiment of the whole nation at that time. Their names, being familiar to nearly all, and accessible to quite all, need not now be repeated.

I take these " thirty-nine," for the present, as being " our fathers who framed the government under which we live." What is the question which, according to the text, those fathers understood " just as well, and even better, than we do now" ?

It is this : Does the proper division of local from Federal authority, or anything in the Constitution, forbid our Federal Government to control as to slavery in our Federal Territories ?

Address at Cooper Institute

Upon this, Senator Douglas holds the affirmative, and Republicans the negative. This affirmation and denial form an issue ; and this issue—this question—is precisely what the text declares our fathers understood '' better than we." Let us now inquire whether the " thirty-nine," or any of them, ever acted upon this question ; and if they did, how they acted upon it—how they expressed that better understanding. In 1784, three years before the Constitution, the United States then owning the Northwestern Territory, and no other, the Congress of the Confederation had before them the question of prohibiting slavery in that Territory : and four of the " thirty-nine" who afterward framed the Constitution were in that Congress, and voted on that question. Of these, Roger Sherman, Thomas Mifflin, and Hugh Williamson voted for the prohibition, thus showing that, in their understanding, no line dividing local from Federal authority, nor anything else, properly forbade the Federal Government to control as to slavery in Federal territory. The other of the four, James McHenry, voted against the prohibition, showing that for some cause he thought it improper to vote for it.

In 1787, still before the Constitution, but while the convention was in session framing it, and while the Northwestern Territory still was the only Territory owned by the United States, the same question of prohibiting slavery in the Territory again came before the Congress of

the Confederation ; and two more of the
" thirty-nine" who afterward signed the Constitution were in that Congress, and voted on the
question.   They were William Blount and William Few ; and they both voted for the prohibition—thus showing that in their understanding no line dividing local from Federal
authority, nor anything else, properly forbade
the Federal Government to control as to slavery
in Federal territory.   This time the prohibition
became a law, being part of what is now well
known as the ordinance of '87.

The question of Federal control of slavery in
the Territories seems not to have been directly
before the convention which framed the original Constitution ; and hence it is not recorded
that the " thirty-nine," or any of them, while
engaged on that instrument, expressed any
opinion on that precise question.

In 1789, by the first Congress which sat under
the Constitution, an act was passed to enforce
the ordinance of '87, including the prohibition
of slavery in the Northwestern Territory.   The
bill for this act was reported by one of the
" thirty-nine"—Thomas Fitzsimmons, then a
member of the House of Representatives from
Pennsylvania.   It went through all its stages
without a word of opposition, and finally passed
both branches without ayes and nays, which is
equivalent to a unanimous passage.   In this
Congress there were sixteen of the thirty-nine
fathers who framed the original Constitution.

Address at Cooper Institute

They were John Langdon, Nicholas Gilman, Wm. S. Johnson, Roger Sherman, Robert Morris, Thos. Fitzsimmons, William Few, Abraham Baldwin, Rufus King, William Paterson, George Clymer, Richard Bassett, George Read, Pierce Butler, Daniel Carroll, and James Madison.

This shows that, in their understanding, no line dividing local from Federal authority, nor anything in the Constitution, properly forbade Congress to prohibit slavery in the Federal territory ; else both their fidelity to correct principle, and their oath to support the Constitution, would have constrained them to oppose the prohibition.

Again, George Washington, another of the "thirty-nine," was then President of the United States, and as such approved and signed the bill, thus completing its validity as a law, and thus showing that, in his understanding, no line dividing local from Federal authority, nor anything in the Constitution, forbade the Federal Government to control as to slavery in Federal territory.

No great while after the adoption of the original Constitution, North Carolina ceded to the Federal Government the country now constituting the State of Tennessee ; and a few years later Georgia ceded that which now constitutes the States of Mississippi and Alabama. In both deeds of cession it was made a condition by the ceding States that the Federal Government should not prohibit slavery in the ceded

Abraham Lincoln

country. Besides this, slavery was then actually in the ceded country. Under these circumstances, Congress, on taking charge of these countries, did not absolutely prohibit slavery within them. But they did interfere with it—take control of it—even there, to a certain extent. In 1798 Congress organized the Territory of Mississippi. In the act of organization they prohibited the bringing of slaves into the Territory from any place without the United States, by fine, and giving freedom to slaves so brought. This act passed both branches of Congress without yeas and nays. In that Congress were three of the "thirty-nine" who framed the original Constitution. They were John Langdon, George Read, and Abraham Baldwin. They all probably voted for it. Certainly they would have placed their opposition to it upon record if, in their understanding, any line dividing local from Federal authority, or anything in the Constitution, properly forbade the Federal Government to control as to slavery in Federal territory.

In 1803 the Federal Government purchased the Louisiana country. Our former territorial acquisitions came from certain of our own States; but this Louisiana country was acquired from a foreign nation. In 1804 Congress gave a territorial organization to that part of it which now constitutes the State of Louisiana. New Orleans, lying within that part, was an old and comparatively large city.

There were other considerable towns and settlements, and slavery was extensively and thoroughly intermingled with the people. Congress did not, in the Territorial Act, prohibit slavery ; but they did interfere with it—take control of it—in a more marked and extensive way than they did in the case of Mississippi. The substance of the provision therein made in relation to slaves was :

1st. That no slave should be imported into the Territory from foreign parts.

2d. That no slave should be carried into it who had been imported into the United States since the first day of May, 1798.

3d. That no slave should be carried into it, except by the owner, and for his own use as a settler ; the penalty in all the cases being a fine upon the violator of the law, and freedom to the slave.

This act also was passed without ayes or nays. In the Congress which passed it there were two of the " thirty-nine." They were Abraham Baldwin and Jonathan Dayton. As stated in the case of Mississippi, it is probable they both voted for it. They would not have allowed it to pass without recording their opposition to it if, in their understanding, it violated either the line properly dividing local from Federal authority, or any provision of the Constitution.

In 1819–20 came and passed the Missouri question. Many votes were taken, by yeas and nays, in both branches of Congress, upon the various phases of the general question. Two of the " thirty-nine"—Rufus King and Charles Pinckney—were members of that Congress. Mr. King steadily voted for slavery prohibition and against all compromises, while Mr. Pinckney as steadily voted against slavery prohibition and against all compromises. By this, Mr. King showed that, in his understanding, no line dividing local from Federal authority, nor anything in the Constitution, was violated by Congress prohibiting slavery in Federal territory ; while Mr. Pinckney, by his votes, showed that, in his understanding, there was some sufficient reason for opposing such prohibition in that case.

The cases I have mentioned are the only acts of the " thirty-nine," or of any of them, upon the direct issue, which I have been able to discover..

To enumerate the persons who thus acted as being four in 1784, two in 1787, seventeen in 1789, three in 1798, two in 1804, and two in 1819–20, there would be thirty of them. But this would be counting John Langdon, Roger Sherman, William Few, Rufus King, and George Read each twice, and Abraham Baldwin three times. The true number of those of the " thirty-nine" whom I have shown to have acted upon the question which, by the text, they understood better than we, is twenty-three, leaving sixteen not shown to have acted upon it in any way.

Address at Cooper Institute

Here, then, we have twenty-three out of our thirty-nine fathers "who framed the government under which we live," who have, upon their official responsibility and their corporal oaths, acted upon the very question which the text affirms they "understood just as well, and even better, than we do now ;" and twenty-one of them—a clear majority of the whole "thirty-nine"—so acting upon it as to make them guilty of gross political impropriety and wilful perjury if, in their understanding, any proper division between local and Federal authority, or anything in the Constitution they had made themselves, and sworn to support, forbade the Federal Government to control as to slavery in the Federal Territories. Thus the twenty-one acted ; and, as actions speak louder than words, so actions under such responsibility speak still louder.

Two of the twenty-three voted against congressional prohibition of slavery in the Federal Territories, in the instances in which they acted upon the question. But for what reasons they so voted is not known. They may have done so because they thought a proper division of local from Federal authority, or some provision or principle of the Constitution, stood in the way ; or they may, without any such question, have voted against the prohibition on what appeared to them to be sufficient grounds of expediency. No one who has sworn to support the Constitution can conscientiously vote for

45

what he understands to be an unconstitutional measure, however expedient he may think it ; but one may and ought to vote against a measure which he deems constitutional if, at the same time, he deems it inexpedient. It, therefore, would be unsafe to set down even the two who voted against the prohibition as having done so because, in their understanding, any proper division of local from Federal authority, or anything in the Constitution, forbade the Federal Government to control as to slavery in Federal territory.

The remaining sixteen of the " thirty-nine," so far as I have discovered, have left no record of their understanding upon the direct question of Federal control of slavery in the Federal Territories. But there is much reason to believe that their understanding upon that question would not have appeared different from that of their twenty-three compeers, had it been manifested at all.

For the purpose of adhering rigidly to the text, I have purposely omitted whatever understanding may have been manifested by any person, however distinguished, other than the thirty-nine fathers who framed the original Constitution ; and, for the same reason, I have also omitted whatever understanding may have been manifested by any of the " thirty-nine" even on any other phase of the general question of slavery. If we should look into their acts and declarations on those other phases, as the foreign slave-trade, and the morality and policy of slavery generally, it would appear to us that on the direct question of Federal control of slavery in Federal Territories, the sixteen, if they had acted at all, would probably have acted just as the twenty-three did. Among that sixteen were several of the most noted anti-slavery men of those times—as Dr. Franklin, Alexander Hamilton, and Gouverneur Morris—while there was not one now known to have been otherwise, unless it may be John Rutledge, of South Carolina.

The sum of the whole is that of our thirty-nine fathers who framed the original Constitution, twenty-one—a clear majority of the whole —certainly understood that no proper division of local from Federal authority, nor any part of the Constitution, forbade the Federal Government to control slavery in the Federal Territories ; while all the rest had probably the same understanding. Such, unquestionably, was the understanding of our fathers who framed the original Constitution ; and the text affirms that they understood the question " better than we."

But, so far, I have been considering the understanding of the question manifested by the framers of the original Constitution. In and by the original instrument, a mode was provided for amending it ; and, as I have already stated, the present frame of " the government under which we live" consists of that original, and twelve amendatory articles framed and adopted since. Those who now insist that Federal control of slavery in Federal Territories violates the Constitution, point us to the provisions which they suppose it thus violates ; and, as I understand, they all fix upon provisions in these amendatory articles, and not in the original instrument. The Supreme Court, in the Dred Scott case, plant themselves upon the fifth amendment, which provides that no person shall be deprived of " life, liberty, or property without due process of law ;" while Senator Douglas and his peculiar adherents plant themselves upon the tenth amendment, providing that " the powers not delegated to the United States by. the Constitution" " are reserved to the States respectively, or to the people."

Now it so happens that these amendments were framed by the first Congress which sat under the Constitution—the identical Congress which passed the act, already mentioned, enforcing the prohibition of slavery in the Northwestern Territory. Not only was it the same Congress, but they were the identical, same individual men who, at the same session, and at the same time within the session, had under consideration, and in progress toward maturity, these constitutional amendments, and this act prohibiting slavery in all the territory the nation then owned. The constitutional amendments were introduced before, and passed after, the act enforcing the ordinance of '87 ; so that, during the whole pendency of the act to enforce the ordinance, the constitutional amendments were also pending.

The seventy-six members of that Congress, including sixteen of the framers of the original Constitution, as before stated, were pre-eminently our fathers who framed that part of " the government under which we live" which is now claimed as forbidding the Federal Government to control slavery in the Federal Territories.

Is it not a little presumptuous in any one at this day to affirm that the two things which that Congress deliberately framed, and carried to maturity at the same time, are absolutely inconsistent with each other? And does not such affirmation become impudently absurd when coupled with the other affirmation, from the same mouth, that those who did the two things alleged to be inconsistent, understood whether they really were inconsistent better than we— better than he who affirms that they are inconsistent?

It is surely safe to assume that the thirty-nine framers of the original Constitution, and the seventy-six members of the Congress which framed the amendments thereto, taken together, do certainly include those who may be fairly called " our fathers who framed the government under which we live." And so assuming, I defy any man to show that any one of them ever, in his whole life, declared that, in his understanding, any proper division of local from Federal authority, or any part of the Constitution, forbade the Federal Government to control as to slavery in the Federal Territories. I go a step further. I defy any one to show that any living man in the whole world ever did, prior to the beginning of the present century (and I might almost say prior to the beginning of the last half of the present century), declare that, in his understanding, any proper division of local from Federal authority, or any part of the Constitution, forbade the Federal Government to control as to slavery in the Federal Territories. To those who now so declare I give not only "our fathers who framed the government under which we live," but with them all other living men within the century in which it was framed, among whom to search, and they shall not be able to find the evidence of a single man agreeing with them.

Now, and here, let me guard a little against being misunderstood. I do not mean to say we are bound to follow implicitly in whatever our fathers did. To do so would be to discard all the lights of current experience—to reject all progress, all improvement. What I do say is that if we would supplant the opinions and policy of our fathers in any case, we should do so upon evidence so conclusive, and argument so clear, that even their great authority, fairly considered and weighed, cannot stand; and most surely not in a case whereof we ourselves declare they understood the question better than we.

If any man at this day sincerely believes that a proper division of local from Federal authority, or any part of the Constitution, forbids the Federal Government to control as to slavery in the Federal Territories, he is right to say so, and to enforce his position by all truthful evidence and fair argument which he can. But he has no right to mislead others, who have less access to history, and less leisure to study it, into the false belief that "our fathers who framed the government under which we live" were of the same opinion—thus substituting falsehood and deception for truthful evidence and fair argument. If any man at this day sincerely believes "our fathers who framed the government under which we live" used and applied principles, in other cases, which ought to have led them to understand that a proper division of local from Federal authority, or some part of the Constitution, forbids the Federal Government to control as to slavery in the Federal Territories, he is right to say so. But he should, at the same time, brave the responsibility of declaring that, in his opinion, he understands their principles better than they did themselves ; and especially should he not shirk that responsibility by asserting that they " understood the question just as well, and even better, than we do now."

But enough ! Let all who believe that "our

fathers who framed the government under which we live understood this question just as well, and even better, than we do now," speak as they spoke, and act as they acted upon it. This is all Republicans ask—all Republicans desire—in relation to slavery. As those fathers marked it, so let it be again marked, as an evil not to be extended, but to be tolerated and protected only because of and so far as its actual presence among us makes that toleration and protection a necessity. Let all the guaranties those fathers gave it be not grudgingly, but fully and fairly, maintained. For this Republicans contend, and with this, so far as I know or believe, they will be content.

And now, if they would listen—as I suppose they will not—I would address a few words to the Southern people.

I would say to them : You consider yourselves a reasonable and a just people ; and I consider that in the general qualities of reason and justice you are not inferior to any other people. Still, when you speak of us Republicans, you do so only to denounce us as reptiles, or, at the best, as no better than outlaws. You will grant a hearing to pirates or murderers, but nothing like it to " Black Republicans." In all your contentions with one another, each of you deems an unconditional condemnation of " Black Republicanism" as the first thing to be attended to. Indeed, such condemnation of us seems to be an indispensable prerequisite—license, so to speak—among you to be admitted or permitted to speak at all. Now can you or not be prevailed upon to pause and to consider whether this is quite just to us, or even to yourselves? Bring forward your charges and specifications, and then be patient long enough to hear us deny or justify.

You say we are sectional. We deny it. That makes an issue ; and the burden of proof is upon you. You produce your proof ; and what is it? Why, that our party has no existence in your section—gets no votes in your section. The fact is substantially true ; but does it prove the issue? If it does, then in case we should, without change of principle, begin to get votes in your section, we should thereby cease to be sectional. You cannot escape this conclusion ; and yet, are you willing to abide by it? If you are, you will probably soon find that we have ceased to be sectional, for we shall get votes in your section this very year. You will then begin to discover, as the truth plainly is, that your proof does not touch the issue. The fact that we get no votes in your section is a fact of your making, and not of ours. And if there be fault in that fact, that fault is primarily yours, and remains so until you show that we repel you by some wrong principle or practice. If we do repel you by any wrong principle or practice, the fault is ours ; but this brings you to where you ought to have started—to a discussion of the right or wrong of our principle. If

our principle, put in practice, would wrong your
section for the benefit of ours, or for any other
object, then our principle, and we with it, are
sectional, and are justly opposed and denounced
as such. Meet us, then, on the question of
whether our principle, put in practice, would
wrong your section ; and so meet us as if it
were possible that something may be said on
our side. Do you accept the challenge? No !
Then you really believe that the principle which
" our fathers who framed the government under which we live" thought so clearly right as
to adopt it, and indorse it again and again,
upon their official oaths, is in fact so clearly
wrong as to demand your condemnation without a moment's consideration.

Some of you delight to flaunt in our faces the
warning against sectional parties given by
Washington in his Farewell Address. Less
than eight years before Washington gave that
warning, he had, as President of the United
States, approved and signed an act of Congress
enforcing the prohibition of slavery in the
Northwestern Territory, which act embodied
the policy of the government upon that subject
up to and at the very moment he penned that
warning ; and about one year after he penned
it, he wrote Lafayette that he considered that
prohibition a wise measure, expressing in the
same connection his hope that we should at
some time have a confederacy of free States.

Bearing this in mind, and seeing that sectionalism has since arisen upon this same subject, is that warning a weapon in your hands against us, or in our hands against you? Could Washington himself speak, would he cast the blame of that sectionalism upon us, who sustain his policy, or upon you, who repudiate it? We respect that warning of Washington, and we commend it to you, together with his example pointing to the right application of it.

But you say you are conservative—eminently conservative—while we are revolutionary, destructive, or something of the sort. What is conservatism? Is it not adherence to the old and tried, against the new and untried? We stick to, contend for, the identical old policy on the point in controversy which was adopted by "our fathers who framed the government under which we live;" while you with one accord reject, and scout, and spit upon that old policy, and insist upon substituting something new. True, you disagree among yourselves as to what that substitute shall be. You are divided on new propositions and plans, but you are unanimous in rejecting and denouncing the old policy of the fathers. Some of you are for reviving the foreign slave-trade; some for a congressional slave code for the Territories; some for Congress forbidding the Territories to prohibit slavery within their limits; some for maintaining slavery in the Territories through the judiciary; some for the "gur-reat pur-rinciple" that "if one man would enslave another, no third man should object," fantastically called "popular sovereignty ;" but never a man among you is in favor of Federal prohibition of slavery in Federal Territories, according to the practice of "our fathers who framed the government under which we live." Not one of all your various plans can show a precedent or an advocate in the century within which our government originated. Consider, then, whether your claim of conservatism for yourselves, and your charge of destructiveness against us, are based on the most clear and stable foundations.

Again, you say we have made the slavery question more prominent than it formerly was. We deny it. We admit that it is more prominent, but we deny that we made it so. It was not we, but you, who discarded the old policy of the fathers. We resisted, and still resist, your innovation ; and thence comes the greater prominence of the question. Would you have that question reduced to its former proportions ? Go back to that old policy. What has been will be again, under the same conditions. If you would have the peace of the old times, re-adopt the precepts and policy of the old times.

You charge that we stir up insurrections among your slaves. We deny it ; and what is your proof? Harper's Ferry ! John Brown !! John Brown was no Republican ; and you have failed to implicate a single Republican in his Harper's Ferry enterprise. If any member of our party is guilty in that matter, you know it, or you do not know it. If you do know it, you are inexcusable for not designating the man and proving the fact. If you do not know it, you are inexcusable for asserting it, and especially for persisting in the assertion after you have tried and failed to make the proof. You need not be told that persisting in a charge which one does not know to be true, is simply malicious slander.

Some of you admit that no Republican designedly aided or encouraged the Harper's Ferry affair, but still insist that our doctrines and declarations necessarily lead to such results. We do not believe it. We know we hold no doctrine, and make no declaration, which were not held to and made by "our fathers who framed the government under which we live." You never dealt fairly by us in relation to this affair. When it occurred, some important State elections were near at hand, and you were in evident glee with the belief that, by charging the blame upon us, you could get an advantage of us in those elections. The elections came, and your expectations were not quite fulfilled. Every Republican man knew that, as to himself at least, your charge was a slander, and he was not much inclined by it to cast his vote in your favor. Republican doctrines and declarations are accompanied with a continual protest against any interference whatever with your slaves, or with you about your slaves. Surely, this does not encourage them to revolt. True, we do, in common with "our fathers who framed the government under which we live," declare our belief that slavery is wrong ; but the slaves do not hear us declare even this. For anything we say or do, the slaves would scarcely know there is a Republican party. I believe they would not, in fact, generally know it but for your misrepresentations of us in their hearing. In your political contests among yourselves, each faction charges the other with sympathy with Black Republicanism ; and then, to give point to the charge, defines Black Republicanism to simply be insurrection, blood, and thunder among the slaves.

Slave insurrections are no more common now than they were before the Republican party was organized. What induced the Southampton insurrection, twenty-eight years ago, in which at least three times as many lives were lost as at Harper's Ferry? You can scarcely stretch your very elastic fancy to the conclusion that Southampton was " got up by Black Republicanism." In the present state of things in the United States, I do not think a general, or even a very extensive, slave insurrection is possible. The indispensable concert of action cannot be attained. The slaves have no means of rapid communication ; nor can incendiary freemen, black or white, supply it. The explosive materials are everywhere in parcels ; but there neither are, nor can be supplied, the in-dispensable connecting trains.

Much is said by Southern people about the affection of slaves for their masters and mis-tresses ; and a part of it, at least, is true. A plot for an uprising could scarcely be devised and communicated to twenty individuals before some one of them, to save the life of a favorite master or mistress, would divulge it. This is the rule ; and the slave revolution in Hayti was not an exception to it, but a case occurring un-der peculiar circumstances. The gunpowder plot of British history, though not connected with slaves, was more in point. In that case, only about twenty were admitted to the secret ; and yet one of them, in his anxiety to save a friend, betrayed the plot to that friend, and, by consequence, averted the calamity. Occasional poisonings from the kitchen, and open or stealthy assassinations in the field, and local re-volts extending to a score or so, will continue to occur as the natural results of slavery ; but no general insurrection of slaves, as I think, can happen in this country for a long time Whoever much fears, or much hopes, for such an event, will be alike disappointed.

In the language of Mr. Jefferson, uttered many years ago, " It is still in our power to direct the process of emancipation and deporta-tion peaceably, and in such slow degrees, as that the evil will wear off insensibly ; and their places be, *pari passu*, filled up by free white laborers. If, on the contrary, it is left to force itself on, human nature must shudder at the prospect held up."

Mr. Jefferson did not mean to say, nor do I, that the power of emancipation is in the Federal Government. He spoke of Virginia ; and, as to the power of emancipation, I speak of the slaveholding States only. The Federal Government, however, as we insist, has the power of restraining the extension of the institution — the power to insure that a slave insurrection shall never occur on any American soil which is now free from slavery.

John Brown's effort was peculiar. It was not a slave insurrection. It was an attempt by white men to get up a revolt among slaves, in which the slaves refused to participate. In fact, it was so absurd that the slaves, with all their ignorance, saw plainly enough it could not succeed. That affair, in its philosophy, corresponds with the many attempts, related in history, at the assassination of kings and emperors. An enthusiast broods over the oppression of a people till he fancies himself commissioned by Heaven to liberate them. He ventures the attempt, which ends in little else than his own execution. Orsini's attempt on Louis Napoleon, and John Brown's attempt at Harper's Ferry, were, in their philosophy, precisely the same. The eagerness to cast blame on old England in the one case, and on New

Address at Cooper Institute

England in the other, does not disprove the sameness of the two things.

And how much would it avail you, if you could, by the use of John Brown, Helper's Book, and the like, break up the Republican organization? Human action can be modified to some extent, but human nature cannot be changed. There is a judgment and a feeling against slavery in this nation, which cast at least a million and a half of votes. You cannot destroy that judgment and feeling—that sentiment—by breaking up the political organization which rallies around it. You can scarcely scatter and disperse an army which has been formed into order in the face of your heaviest fire; but if you could, how much would you gain by forcing the sentiment which created it out of the peaceful channel of the ballot-box into some other channel? What would that other channel probably be? Would the number of John Browns be lessened or enlarged by the operation?

But you will break up the Union rather than submit to a denial of your constitutional rights.

That has a somewhat reckless sound; but it would be palliated, if not fully justified, were we proposing, by the mere force of numbers, to deprive you of some right plainly written down in the Constitution. But we are proposing no such thing.

When you make these declarations you have

a specific and well-understood allusion to an assumed constitutional right of yours to take slaves into the Federal Territories, and to hold them there as property. But no such right is specially written in the Constitution. That instrument is literally silent about any such right. We, on the contrary, deny that such a right has any existence in the Constitution, even by implication.

Your purpose, then, plainly stated, is that you will destroy the government, unless you be allowed to construe and force the Constitution as you please, on all points in dispute between you and us. You will rule or ruin in all events.

This, plainly stated, is your language. Perhaps you will say the Supreme Court has decided the disputed constitutional question in your favor. Not quite so. But waiving the lawyer's distinction between dictum and decision, the court has decided the question for you in a sort of way. The court has substantially said, it is your constitutional right to take slaves into the Federal Territories, and to hold them there as property. When I say the decision was made in a sort of way, I mean it was made in a divided court, by a bare majority of the judges, and they not quite agreeing with one another in the reasons for making it ; that it is so made as that its avowed supporters disagree with one another about its meaning, and that it was mainly based upon a mistaken statement of fact—the statement in the opinion that

" the right of property in a slave is distinctly and expressly affirmed in the Constitution."

An inspection of the Constitution will show that the right of property in a slave is not " distinctly and expressly affirmed " in it. Bear in mind, the judges do not pledge their judicial opinion that such right is impliedly affirmed in the Constitution ; but they pledge their veracity that it is " distinctly and expressly" affirmed there—" distinctly," that is, not mingled with anything else—" expressly," that is, in words meaning just that, without the aid of any inference, and susceptible of no other meaning.

If they had only pledged their judicial opinion that such right is affirmed in the instrument by implication, it would be open to others to show that neither the word " slave" nor " slavery" is to be found in the Constitution, nor the word " property" even, in any connection with language alluding to the thing slave, or slavery ; and that wherever in that instrument the slave is alluded to, he is called a " person ;" and wherever his master's legal right in relation to him is alluded to, it is spoken of as " service or labor which may be due"—as a debt payable in service or labor. Also it would be open to show, by contemporaneous history, that this mode of alluding to slaves and slavery, instead of speaking of them, was employed on purpose to exclude from the Constitution the idea that there could be property in man.

To show all this is easy and certain.

When this obvious mistake of the judges shall be brought to their notice, is it not reasonable to expect that they will withdraw the mistaken statement, and reconsider the conclusion based upon it?

And then it is to be remembered that "our fathers who framed the government under which we live"—the men who made the Constitution—decided this same constitutional question in our favor long ago : decided it without division among themselves when making the decision ; without division among themselves about the meaning of it after it was made, and, so far as any evidence is left, without basing it upon any mistaken statement of facts.

Under all these circumstances, do you really feel yourselves justified to break up this government unless such a court decision as yours is shall be at once submitted to as a conclusive and final rule of political action? But you will not abide the election of a Republican president! In that supposed event, you say, you will destroy the Union ; and then, you say, the great crime of having destroyed it will be upon us! That is cool. A highwayman holds a pistol to my ear, and mutters through his teeth, "Stand and deliver, or I shall kill you, and then you will be a murderer!"

To be sure, what the robber demanded of me—my money—was my own ; and I had a clear right to keep it ; but it was no more my own than my vote is my own ; and the threat of death to me, to extort my money, and the threat of destruction to the Union, to extort my vote, can scarcely be distinguished in principle.

A few words now to Republicans. It is exceedingly desirable that all parts of this great Confederacy shall be at peace, and in harmony one with another. Let us Republicans do our part to have it so. Even though much provoked, let us do nothing through passion and ill temper. Even though the Southern people will not so much as listen to us, let us calmly consider their demands, and yield to them if, in our deliberate view of our duty, we possibly can. Judging by all they say and do, and by the subject and nature of their controversy with us, let us determine, if we can, what will satisfy them.

Will they be satisfied if the Territories be unconditionally surrendered to them ? We know they will not. In all their present complaints against us, the Territories are scarcely mentioned. Invasions and insurrections are the rage now. Will it satisfy them if, in the future, we have nothing to do with invasions and insurrections ? We know it will not. We so know, because we know we never had anything to do with invasions and insurrections ; and yet this total abstaining does not exempt us from the charge and the denunciation.

The question recurs, What will satisfy them ? Simply this : we must not only let them alone, but we must somehow convince them that we do let them alone. This, we know by experience, is no easy task. We have been so trying to convince them from the very beginning of our organization, but with no success. In all our platforms and speeches we have constantly protested our purpose to let them alone ; but this has had no tendency to convince them. Alike unavailing to convince them is the fact that they have never detected a man of us in any attempt to disturb them.

These natural and apparently adequate means all failing, what will convince them ? This, and this only : cease to call slavery wrong, and join them in calling it right. And this must be done thoroughly—done in acts as well as in words. Silence will not be tolerated—we must place ourselves avowedly with them. Senator Douglas's new sedition law must be enacted and enforced, suppressing all declarations that slavery is wrong, whether made in politics, in presses, in pulpits, or in private. We must arrest and return their fugitive slaves with greedy pleasure. We must pull down our free-State constitutions. The whole atmosphere must be disinfected from all taint of opposition to slavery, before they will cease to believe that all their troubles proceed from us.

I am quite aware they do not state their case precisely in this way. Most of them would probably say to us, " Let us alone ; do nothing to us, and say what you please about slavery."

Address at Cooper Institute

But we do let them alone—have never disturbed them—so that, after all, it is what we say which dissatisfies them. They will continue to accuse us of doing, until we cease saying.

I am also aware they have not as yet in terms demanded the overthrow of our free-State constitutions. Yet those constitutions declare the wrong of slavery with more solemn emphasis than do all other sayings against it ; and when all these other sayings shall have been silenced, the overthrow of these constitutions will be demanded, and nothing be left to resist the demand. It is nothing to the contrary that they do not demand the whole of this just now. Demanding what they do, and for the reason they do, they can voluntarily stop nowhere short of this consummation. Holding, as they do, that slavery is morally right and socially elevating, they cannot cease to demand a full national recognition of it as a legal right and a social blessing.

Nor can we justifiably withhold this on any ground save our conviction that slavery is wrong. If slavery is right, all words, acts, laws, and constitutions against it are themselves wrong, and should be silenced and swept away. If it is right, we cannot justly object to its nationality—its universality ; if it is wrong, they cannot justly insist upon its extension—its enlargement. All they ask we could readily grant, if we thought slavery right ; all we ask they could as readily grant, if they thought it

wrong. Their thinking it right and our thinking it wrong is the precise fact upon which depends the whole controversy. Thinking it
right, as they do, they are not to blame for de-
siring its full recognition as being right ; but
thinking it wrong, as we do, can we yield to
them ? Can we cast our votes with their view,
and against our own ? In view of our moral,
social, and political responsibilities, can we do
this ?

Wrong as we think slavery is, we can yet
afford to let it alone where it is, because that
much is due to the necessity arising from its
actual presence in the nation ; but can we,
while our votes will prevent it, allow it to
spread into the national Territories, and to
overrun us here in these free States? If our
sense of duty forbids this, then let us stand by
our duty fearlessly and effectively. Let us be
diverted by none of those sophistical contrivances wherewith we are so industriously plied
and belabored—contrivances such as groping
for some middle ground between the right and
the wrong : vain as the search for a man who
should be neither a living man nor a dead
man ; such as a policy of " don't care" on a
question about which all true men do care ;
such as Union appeals beseeching true Union
men to yield to Disunionists, reversing the
divine rule, and calling, not the sinners, but
the righteous to repentance ; such as invoca-
tions to Washington, imploring men to unsay

Address at Cooper Institute

what Washington said and undo what Washington did.

Neither let us be slandered from our duty by false accusations against us, nor frightened from it by menaces of destruction to the government, nor of dungeons to ourselves. Let us have faith that right makes might, and in that faith let us to the end dare to do our duty as we understand it.

Farewell at Springfield

February 11, 1861

[These words, to which subsequent events have given an added note of solemnity, were spoken to a vast audience of Lincoln's fellow-citizens upon the rainy February day when he left Springfield for Washington to assume the duties of the Presidency.]

My Friends: No one, not in my situation, can appreciate my feeling of sadness at this parting. To this place, and the kindness of these people, I owe everything. Here I have lived a quarter of a century, and have passed from a young to an old man. Here my children have been born, and one is buried. I now leave, not knowing when or whether ever I may return, with a task before me greater than that which rested upon Washington. Without the assistance of that Divine Being who ever attended him, I cannot succeed. With that assistance, I cannot fail. Trusting in Him who can go with me, and remain with you, and be everywhere for good, let us confidently hope that all will yet be well. To His care commending you, as I hope in your prayers you will commend me, I bid you an affectionate farewell.

Speech in Independence Hall, Philadelphia

February 22, 1861

[During the journey to Washington Lincoln made many brief addresses. The following, spoken in Independence Hall, Philadelphia, upon Washington's Birthday, is one of the most felicitous, and the time and place of its delivery give it additional interest.]

Mr. Cuyler : I am filled with deep emotion at finding myself standing in this place, where were collected together the wisdom, the patriotism, the devotion to principle, from which sprang the institutions under which we live. You have kindly suggested to me that in my hands is the task of restoring peace to our distracted country. I can say in return, sir, that all the political sentiments I entertain have been drawn, so far as I have been able to draw them, from the sentiments which originated in and were given to the world from this hall. I have never had a feeling, politically, that did not spring from the sentiments embodied in the Declaration of Independence. I have often pondered over the dangers which were incurred by the men who assembled here and framed

Abraham Lincoln

and adopted that Declaration. I have pondered over the toils that were endured by the
officers and soldiers of the army who achieved
that independence. I have often inquired of
myself what great principle or idea it was that
kept this Confederacy so long together. It was
not the mere matter of separation of the colonies from the motherland, but that sentiment
in the Declaration of Independence which gave
liberty not alone to the people of this country,
but hope to all the world, for all future time.
It was that which gave promise that in due
time the weights would be lifted from the shoulders of all men, and that all should have an
equal chance. This is the sentiment embodied
in the Declaration of Independence. Now, my
friends, can this country be saved on that
basis? If it can, I will consider myself one of
the happiest men in the world if I can help to
save it. If it cannot be saved upon that principle, it will be truly awful. But if this country
cannot be saved without giving up that principle, I was about to say I would rather be assas-
sinated on this spot than surrender it. Now,
in my view of the present aspect of affairs,
there is no need of bloodshed and war. There
is no necessity for it. I am not in favor of such
a course ; and I may say in advance that there
will be no bloodshed unless it is forced upon
the government. The government will not use
force, unless force is used against it.

My friends, this is wholly an unprepared

Speech in Independence Hall

speech. I did not expect to be called on to say a word when I came here. I supposed I was merely to do something toward raising a flag. I may, therefore, have said something indiscreet. [Cries of " No, no."] But I have said nothing but what I am willing to live by, and, if it be the pleasure of Almighty God, to die by.

First Inaugural Address.

March 4, 1861.

["Mr. Lincoln was simply introduced by Senator Baker, of Oregon, and delivered his inaugural address. His voice had great carrying capacity, and the vast crowd heard with ease a speech of which every sentence was fraught with an importance and scrutinized with an anxiety far beyond that of any other speech ever delivered in the United States. . . . The inaugural address was simple, earnest, and direct, unincumbered by that rhetorical ornamentation which the American people have always admired as the highest form of eloquence. Those Northerners who had expected magniloquent periods and exaggerated outbursts of patriotism were disappointed, and as they listened in vain for the scream of the eagle, many grumbled at the absence of what they conceived to be *force.* Yet the general feeling was of satisfaction, which grew as the address was more thoroughly studied." — *Morse's "Abraham Lincoln."*]

Fellow-citizens of the United States: In compliance with a custom as old as the government itself, I appear before you to address you briefly, and to take in your presence the oath prescribed by the Constitution of the United States to be taken by the President " before he enters on the execution of his office."

First Inaugural Address

I do not consider it necessary at present for me to discuss those matters of administration about which there is no special anxiety or excitement.

Apprehension seems to exist among the people of the Southern States that by the accession of a Republican administration their property and their peace and personal security are to be endangered. There has never been any reasonable cause for such apprehension. Indeed, the most ample evidence to the contrary has all the while existed and been open to their inspection. It is found in nearly all the published speeches of him who now addresses you. I do but quote from one of those speeches when I declare that " I have no purpose, directly or indirectly, to interfere with the institution of slavery in the States where it exists. I believe I have no lawful right to do so, and I have no inclination to do so." Those who nominated and elected me did so with full knowledge that I had made this and many similar declarations, and had never recanted them. And, more than this, they placed in the platform for my acceptance, and as a law to themselves and to me, the clear and emphatic resolution which I now read :

" *Resolved*, That the maintenance inviolate of the rights of the States, and especially the right of each State to order and control its own domestic institutions according to its own judgment exclusively, is essential to that balance of power on which the perfection and endurance of our political fabric depend, and we denounce the lawless invasion by armed force of the soil of any State or Territory, no matter under what pretext, as among the gravest of crimes.''

I now reiterate these sentiments; and, in doing so, I only press upon the public attention the most conclusive evidence of which the case is susceptible, that the property, peace, and security of no section are to be in any wise endangered by the now incoming administration. I add, too, that all the protection which, consistently with the Constitution and the laws, can be given, will be cheerfully given to all the States when lawfully demanded, for whatever cause—as cheerfully to one section as to another.

There is much controversy about the delivering up of fugitives from service or labor. The clause I now read is as plainly written in the Constitution as any other of its provisions:

'' No person held to service or labor in one State, under the laws thereof, escaping into another, shall in consequence of any law or regulation therein be discharged from such service or labor, but shall be delivered up on claim of the party to whom such service or labor may be due.''

It is scarcely questioned that this provision was intended by those who made it for the reclaiming of what we call fugitive slaves; and the intention of the lawgiver is the law. All members of Congress swear their support to the whole Constitution—to this provision as much as to any other. To the proposition, then, that slaves whose cases come within the terms of this clause " shall be delivered up," their oaths are unanimous. Now, if they would make the effort in good temper, could they not with nearly equal unanimity frame and pass a law by means of which to keep good that unanimous oath ?

There is some difference of opinion whether this clause should be enforced by national or by State authority ; but surely that difference is not a very material one. If the slave is to be surrendered, it can be of but little consequence to him or to others by which authority it is done. And should any one in any case be content that his oath shall go unkept on a merely unsubstantial controversy as to how it shall be kept ?

Again, in any law upon this subject, ought not all the safeguards of liberty known in civilized and humane jurisprudence to be introduced, so that a free man be not, in any case, surrendered as a slave ? And might it not be well at the same time to provide by law for the enforcement of that clause in the Constitution which guarantees that "the citizen of each State shall be entitled to all privileges and immunities of citizens in the several States" ?

I take the official oath to-day with no mental reservations, and with no purpose to construe the Constitution or laws by any hypercritical rules. And while I do not choose now to specify

particular acts of Congress as proper to be enforced, I do suggest that it will be much safer
for all, both in official and private stations, to
conform to and abide by all those acts which
stand unrepealed, than to violate any of them,
trusting to find impunity in having them held
to be unconstitutional.

It is seventy-two years since the first inauguration of a President under our National Constitution. During that period fifteen different
and greatly distinguished citizens have, in suc-
cession, administered the executive branch of
the government. They have conducted it
through many perils, and generally with great
success. Yet, with all this scope of precedent,
I now enter upon the same task for the brief
constitutional term of four years under great
and peculiar difficulty. A disruption of the
Federal Union, heretofore only menaced, is
now formidably attempted.

I hold that, in contemplation of universal law
and of the Constitution, the Union of these
States is perpetual. Perpetuity is implied, if
not expressed, in the fundamental law of all
national governments. It is safe to assert that
no government proper ever had a provision in
its organic law for its own termination. Continue to execute all the express provisions of
our National Constitution, and the Union will
endure forever—it being impossible to destroy
it except by some action not provided for in the
instrument itself.

First Inaugural Address

Again, if the United States be not a government proper, but an association of States in the nature of contract merely, can it, as a contract, be peaceably unmade by less than all the parties who made it? One party to a contract may violate it—break it, so to speak ; but does it not require all to lawfully rescind it ?

Descending from these general principles, we find the proposition that, in legal contemplation the Union is perpetual confirmed by the history of the Union itself. The Union is much older than the Constitution. It was formed, in fact, by the Articles of Association in 1774. It was matured and continued by the Declaration of Independence in 1776. It was further matured, and the faith of all the then thirteen States expressly plighted and engaged that it should be perpetual, by the Articles of Confederation in 1778. And, finally, in 1787 one of the declared objects for ordaining and establishing the Constitution was " to form a more perfect Union."

But if the destruction of the Union by one or by a part only of the States be lawfully possible, the Union is less perfect than before the Constitution, having lost the vital element of perpetuity.

It follows from these views that no State upon its own mere motion can lawfully get out of the Union ; that resolves and ordinances to that effect are legally void ; and that acts of violence, within any State or States, against the authority of the United States, are insurrectionary or revolutionary, according to circumstances.

I therefore consider that, in view of the Constitution and the laws, the Union is unbroken ;
and to the extent of my ability I shall take care,
as the Constitution itself expressly enjoins upon
me, that the laws of the Union be faithfully
executed in all the States. Doing this I deem
to be only a simple duty on my part ; and I
shall perform it so far as practicable, unless my
rightful masters, the American people, shall
withhold the requisite means, or in some authoritative manner direct the contrary. I trust
this will not be regarded as a menace, but only
as the declared purpose of the Union that it
will constitutionally defend and maintain itself.

In doing this there needs to be no bloodshed
or violence ; and there shall be none, unless it
be forced upon the national authority. The
power confided to me will be used to hold, occupy, and possess the property and places belonging to the government, and to collect the
duties and imposts ; but beyond what may be
necessary for these objects, there will be no invasion, no using of force against or among the
people anywhere. Where hostility to the
United States, in any interior locality, shall be
so great and universal as to prevent competent
resident citizens from holding the Federal
offices, there will be no attempt to force obnoxious strangers among the people for that object,

First Inaugural Address

While the strict legal right may exist in the government to enforce the exercise of these offices, the attempt to do so would be so irritating, and so nearly impracticable withal, that I deem it better to forego for the time the uses of such offices.

The mails, unless repelled, will continue to be furnished in all parts of the Union. So far as possible, the people everywhere shall have that sense of perfect security which is most favorable to calm thought and reflection. The course here indicated will be followed unless current events and experience shall show a modification or change to be proper, and in every case and exigency my best discretion will be exercised according to circumstances actually existing, and with a view and a hope of a peaceful solution of the national troubles and the restoration of fraternal sympathies and affections.

That there are persons in one section or another who seek to destroy the Union at all events, and are glad of any pretext to do it, I will neither affirm nor deny ; but if there be such, I need address no word to them. To those, however, who really love the Union may I not speak ?

Before entering upon so grave a matter as the destruction of our national fabric, with all its benefits, its memories, and its hopes, would it not be wise to ascertain precisely why we do it ? Will you hazard so desperate a step while there is any possibility that any portion of the ills you fly from have no real existence? Will you, while the certain ills you fly to are greater than all the real ones you fly from—will you risk the commission of so fearful a mistake?

All profess to be content in the Union if all constitutional rights can be maintained. Is it true, then, that any right, plainly written in the Constitution, has been denied? I think not. Happily the human mind is so constituted that no party can reach to the audacity of doing this. Think, if you can, of a single instance in which a plainly written provision of the Constitution has ever been denied. If by the mere force of numbers a majority should deprive a minority of any clearly written constitutional right, it might, in a moral point of view, justify revolution—certainly would if such a right were a vital one. But such is not our case. All the vital rights of minorities and of individuals are so plainly assured to them by affirmations and negations, guarantees and prohibitions, in the Constitution, that controversies never arise concerning them. But no organic law can ever be framed with a provision specifically applicable to every question which may occur in practical administration. No foresight can anticipate, nor any document of reasonable length contain, express provisions for all possible questions. Shall fugitives from labor be surrendered by national or by State authority? The Constitution does not expressly say. *May* Congress prohibit slavery in the Territories? The Constitution does not expressly say. *Must* Congress protect slavery in the Territories? The Constitution does not expressly say.

From questions of this class spring all our constitutional controversies, and we divide upon them into majorities and minorities. If the minority will not acquiesce, the majority must, or the government must cease. There is no other alternative ; for continuing the government is acquiescence on one side or the other.

If a minority in such case will secede rather than acquiesce, they make a precedent which in turn will divide and ruin them ; for a minority of their own will secede from them whenever a majority refuses to be controlled by such minority. For instance, why may not any portion of a new confederacy a year or two hence arbitrarily secede again, precisely as portions of the present Union now claim to secede from it? All who cherish disunion sentiments are now being educated to the exact temper of doing this.

Is there such perfect identity of interests among the States to compose a new Union, as to produce harmony only, and prevent renewed secession?

Plainly, the central idea of secession is the essence of anarchy. A majority held in restraint by constitutional checks and limitations, and always changing easily with deliberate changes of popular opinions and sentiments, is the only true sovereign of a free people. Who-

ever rejects it does, of necessity, fly to anarchy
or to despotism. Unanimity is impossible ; the
rule of a minority, as a permanent arrange-
ment, is wholly inadmissible ; so that, rejecting
the majority principle, anarchy or despotism in
some form is all that is left.

I do not forget the position, assumed by some,
that constitutional questions are to be decided
by the Supreme Court ; nor do I deny that such
decisions must be binding, in any case, upon
the parties to a suit, as to the object of that suit,
while they are also entitled to very high respect
and consideration in all parallel cases by all
other departments of the government. And
while it is obviously possible that such decision
may be erroneous in any given case, still the
evil effect following it, being limited to that
particular case, with the chance that it may be
overruled and never become a precedent for
other cases, can better be borne than could the
evils of a different practice. At the same time,
the candid citizen must confess that if the policy of the government, upon vital questions
affecting the whole people, is to be irrevocably
fixed by decisions of the Supreme Court, the
instant they are made, in ordinary litigation
between parties in personal actions, the people
will have ceased to be their own rulers, having
to that extent practically resigned their government into the hands of that eminent tribunal.
Nor is there in this view any assault upon the
court or the judges. It is a duty from which

First Inaugural Address

they may not shrink to decide cases properly
brought before them, and it is no fault of theirs
if others seek to turn their decisions to political
purposes.

One section of our country believes slavery
is right, and ought to be extended, while the
other believes it is wrong, and ought not to be
extended.   This is the only substantial dispute.
The fugitive-slave clause of the Constitution,
and the law for the suppression of the foreign
slave-trade, are each as well enforced, perhaps,
as any law can ever be in a community where
the moral sense of the people imperfectly sup-
ports the law itself.   The great body of the
people abide by the dry legal obligation in both
cases, and a few break over in each.   This, I
think, cannot be perfectly cured ; and it would
be worse in both cases after the separation of
the sections than before.   The foreign slave-
trade, now imperfectly suppressed, would be
ultimately revived, without restriction, in one
section, while fugitive slaves, now only partially
surrendered, would not be surrendered at all
by the other.

Physically speaking, we cannot separate.
We cannot remove our respective sections from
each other, nor build an impassable wall between them.   A husband and wife may be
divorced, and go out of the presence and beyond the reach of each other ; but the different
parts of our country cannot do this.   They cannot but remain face to face, and intercourse,

either amicable or hostile, must continue between them. Is it possible, then, to make that intercourse more advantageous or more satisfactory after separation than before? Can aliens make treaties easier than friends can make laws? Can treaties be more faithfully enforced between aliens than laws can among friends? Suppose you go to war, you cannot fight always; and when, after much loss on both sides, and no gain on either, you cease fighting, the identical old questions as to terms of intercourse are again upon you.

This country, with its institutions, belongs to the people who inhabit it. Whenever they shall grow weary of the existing government, they can exercise their constitutional right of amending it, or their revolutionary right to dismember or overthrow it. I cannot be ignorant of the fact that many worthy and patriotic citizens are desirous of having the National Constitution amended. While I make no recommendation of amendments, I fully recognize the rightful authority of the people over the whole subject, to be exercised in either of the modes prescribed in the instrument itself; and I should, under existing circumstances, favor rather than oppose a fair opportunity being afforded the people to act upon it. I will venture to add that to me the convention mode seems preferable, in that it allows amendments to originate with the people themselves, instead of only permitting them to take or reject propositions originated by others not especially chosen for the purpose, and which might not be precisely such as they would wish to either accept or refuse. I understand a proposed amendment to the Constitution—which amendment, however, I have not seen—has passed Congress, to the effect that the Federal Government shall never interfere with the domestic institutions of the States, including that of persons held to service. To avoid misconstruction of what I have said, I depart from my purpose not to speak of particular amendments so far as to say that, holding such a provision to now be implied constitutional law, I have no objection to its being made express and irrevocable.

The chief magistrate derives all his authority from the people, and they have conferred none upon him to fix terms for the separation of the States. The people themselves can do this also if they choose ; but the executive, as such, has nothing to do with it. His duty is to administer the present government, as it came to his hands, and to transmit it, unimpaired by him, to his successor.

Why should there not be a patient confidence in the ultimate justice of the people ? Is there any better or equal hope in the world ? In our present differences is either party without faith of being in the right ? If the Almighty Ruler of Nations, with his eternal truth and justice, be on your side of the North, or on yours of the South, that truth and that justice will surely prevail by the judgment of this great tribunal of the American people.

By the frame of the government under which we live, this same people have wisely given their public servants but little power for mischief ; and have, with equal wisdom, provided for the return of that little to their own hands at very short intervals. While the people retain their virtue and vigilance, no administration, by any extreme of wickedness or folly, can very seriously injure the government in the short space of four years.

My countrymen, one and all, think calmly and well upon this whole subject. Nothing valuable can be lost by taking time. If there be an object to hurry any of you in hot haste to a step which you would never take deliberately, that object will be frustrated by taking time ; but no good object can be frustrated by it. Such of you as are now dissatisfied, still have the old Constitution unimpaired, and, on the sensitive point, the laws of your own framing under it ; while the new administration will have no immediate power, if it would, to change either. If it were admitted that you who are dissatisfied hold the right side in the dispute, there still is no single good reason for precipitate action. Intelligence, patriotism, Christianity, and a firm reliance on Him who has never yet forsaken this favored land, are still competent to adjust in the best way all our present difficulty.

First Inaugural Address

In your hands, my dissatisfied fellow-countrymen, and not in mine, is the momentous issue of civil war. The government will not assail you. You can have no conflict without being yourselves the aggressors. You have no oath registered in heaven to destroy the government, while I shall have the most solemn one to " preserve, protect, and defend it."

I am loath to close. We are not enemies, but friends. We must not be enemies. Though passion may have strained, it must not break our bonds of affection. The mystic chords of memory, stretching from every battle-field and patriot grave to every living heart and hearth-stone all over this broad land, will yet swell the chorus of the Union when again touched, as surely they will be, by the better angels of our nature.

Emancipation Proclamation

January 1, 1863

BY THE PRESIDENT OF THE UNITED STATES O
AMERICA :

A Proclamation

Whereas, on the twenty-second day of Sep
tember, in the year of our Lord one thousan
eight hundred and sixty-two, a proclamatio
was issued by the President of the Unite
States, containing, among other things, the fo
lowing, to wit :

" That on the first day of January, in th
year of our Lord one thousand eight hundre
and sixty-three, all persons held as slaves withi
any State, or designated part of a State, tl
people whereof shall then be in rebellion again
the United States, shall be then, thenceforwar·
and forever free ; and the Executive Gover
ment of the United States, including the mi
tary and naval authority thereof, will recogni
and maintain the freedom of such person.   nd
will do no act or acts to repress such pers ns,
or any of them, in any efforts they may make
for their actual freedom.

" That the Executive will, on the first day of

January aforesaid, by proclamation, designate
the States and parts of States, if any, in which
the people thereof respectively shall then be in
ebellion against the United States ; and the
act that any State, or the people thereof, shall
m that day be in good faith represented in the
Congress of the United States by members
·hosen thereto at elections wherein a majority
)f the qualified voters of such State shall have
)articipated, shall in the absence of strong
:ountervailing testimony be deemed conclusive
:vidence that such State and the people thereof
ire not then in rebellion against the United
States."

Now, therefore, I, Abraham Lincoln, Presi-
lent of the United States, by virtue of the
)ower in me vested as commander-in-chief of
he army and navy of the United States, in
ime of actual armed rebellion against the au-
hority and government of the United States,
nd as a fit and necessary war measure for suppressing said rebellion, do, on this first day of
anuary, in the year of our Lord one thousand
ight hundred and sixty-three, and in accord-
nce with my purpose so to do, publicly pro-
laimed for the full period of 100 days from the
ay first above mentioned, order and designate
s the States and parts of States wherein the
people thereof, respectively, are this day in rebellion against the United States, the following, to wit :

Arkansas, Texas, Louisiana (except the parishes of St. Bernard, Plaquemines, Jefferson, St. John, St. Charles, St. James, Ascension, Assumption, Terre Bonne, Lafourche, St. Mary, St. Martin, and Orleans, including the city of New Orleans), Mississippi, Alabama, Florida, Georgia, South Carolina, North Carolina, and Virginia (except the forty-eight counties designated as West Virginia, and also the counties of Berkeley, Accomac, Northampton, Elizabeth City, York, Princess Ann, and Norfolk, including the cities of Norfolk and Portsmouth), and which excepted parts are for the present left precisely as if this proclamation were not issued.

And by virtue of the power and for the purpose aforesaid, I do order and declare that all persons held as slaves within said designated States and parts of States are, and henceforward shall be, free ; and that the Executive Government of the United States, including the military and naval authorities thereof, will recognize and maintain the freedom of said persons.

And I hereby enjoin upon the people so declared to be free to abstain from all violence, unless in necessary self-defence ; and I recommend to them that, in all cases when allowed, they labor faithfully for reasonable wages.

And I further declare and make known that such persons of suitable condition will be received into the armed service of the United States to garrison forts, positions, stations, and

Emancipation Proclamation

other places, and to man vessels of all sorts in said service.

And upon this act, sincerely believed to be an act of justice, warranted by the Constitution upon military necessity, I invoke the considerate judgment of mankind and the gracious favor of Almighty God.

In witness whereof, I have hereunto set my hand, and caused the seal of the United States to be affixed.

[L. S.]   Done at the city of Washington, this first day of January, in the year of our Lord one thousand eight hundred and sixty-three, and of the independence of the United States of America the eighty-seventh.

ABRAHAM LINCOLN.

By the President : WILLIAM H. SEWARD, Secretary of State.

.

Gettysburg Address

November 19, 1863

[The national military cemetery at Gettysburg, Pa., was dedicated with solemn ceremo-
nies on November 19, 1863, as a memorial of
the three days' battle fought in the previous
July, which proved to be the turning-point of
the Civil War. The formal oration of the day
was pronounced by Edward Everett, but the
President was asked to add a word. His biog-
rapher, Mr. J. G. Nicolay, has given an interesting account of the preparation of the address.
(*Century Magazine*, Vol. XLVII.) It was delivered without any effort at oratorical effect ;
but its perfection of feeling and of phrase was
instantly and universally recognized. To have
composed the Gettysburg address is proof
enough, were there no other, of Lincoln's place
among the masters of English speech. His letter to Edward Everett acknowledging the latter's praise, and complimenting Everett in turn,
is included in this volume of selections.]

FOURSCORE and seven years ago our fathers
brought forth on this continent a new nation,
conceived in liberty, and dedicated to the proposition that all men are created equal.

Now we are engaged in a great civil war,
testing whether that nation, or any nation so

conceived and so dedicated, can long endure.
We are met on a great battle-field of that war.
We have come to dedicate a portion of that field
as a final resting-place for those who here gave
their lives that that nation might live. It is
altogether fitting and proper that we should do
this.

But, in a larger sense, we cannot dedicate—
we cannot consecrate—we cannot hallow—this
ground. The brave men, living and dead, who
struggled here, have consecrated it far above
our poor power to add or detract. The world
will little note nor long remember what we say
here, but it can never forget what they did
here. It is for us, the living, rather, to be dedicated here to the unfinished work which they
who fought here have thus far so nobly ad-
vanced. It is rather for us to be here dedicated
to the great task remaining before us—that
from these honored dead we take increased devotion to that cause for which they gave the
last full measure of devotion ; that we here
highly resolve that these dead shall not have
died in vain ; that this nation, under God, shall
have a new birth of freedom ; and that government of the people, by the people, for the people, shall not perish from the earth.

Speech to 166th Ohio Regiment

August 22, 1864

Soldiers: I suppose you are going home to see your families and friends. For the services you have done in this great struggle in which we are all engaged, I present you sincere thanks for myself and the country.

I almost always feel inclined, when I happen to say anything to soldiers, to impress upon them, in a few brief remarks, the importance of success in this contest. It is not merely for to-day, but for all time to come, that we should perpetuate for our children's children that great and free government which we have enjoyed all our lives. I beg you to remember this, not merely for my sake, but for yours. I happen, temporarily, to occupy this White House. I am a living witness that any one of your children may look to come here as my father's child has. It is in order that each one of you may have, through this free government which we have enjoyed, an open field and a fair chance for your industry, enterprise, and intelligence ; that you may all have equal privileges in the race of life, with all its desirable human aspira-

Speech to 166th Ohio Regiment

tions. It is for this the struggle should be
maintained, that we may not lose our birthright
—not only for one, but for two or three years.
The nation is worth fighting for, to secure such
an inestimable jewel.

Response to Serenade

November 10, 1864

[This little speech was called forth by the news of Lincoln's re-election as President.]

It has long been a grave question whether any government, not too strong for the liberties of its people, can be strong enough to maintain its existence in great emergencies. On this point the present rebellion brought our republic to a severe test, and a presidential election occurring in regular course during the rebellion, added not a little to the strain.

If the loyal people united were put to the utmost of their strength by the rebellion, must they not fail when divided and partially paralyzed by a political war among themselves? But the election was a necessity. We cannot have free government without elections ; and if the rebellion could force us to forego or postpone a national election, it might fairly claim to have already conquered and ruined us. The strife of the election is but human nature practically applied to the facts of the case. What has occurred in this case must ever recur in similar cases. Human nature will not change. In any future great national trial, compared

Response to Serenade

with the men of this, we shall have as weak and as strong, as silly and as wise, as bad and as good. Let us, therefore, study the incidents of this as philosophy to learn wisdom from, and none of them as wrongs to be revenged. But the election, along with its incidental and undesirable strife, has done good too. It has demonstrated that a people's government can sustain a national election in the midst of a great civil war. Until now, it has not been known to the world that this was a possibility. It shows, also, how sound and how strong we still are. It shows that, even among candidates of the same party, he who is most devoted to the Union and most opposed to treason can receive most of the people's votes. It shows, also, to the extent yet known, that we have more men now than we had when the war began. Gold is good in its place, but living, brave, patriotic men are better than gold.

But the rebellion continues, and now that the election is over, may not all having a common interest reunite in a common effort to save our common country? For my own part, I have striven and shall strive to avoid placing any obstacle in the way. So long as I have been here I have not willingly planted a thorn in any man's bosom. While I am deeply sensible to the high compliment of a re-election, and duly grateful, as I trust, to Almighty God for having directed my countrymen to a right conclusion, as I think, for their own good, it adds nothing to my satisfaction that any other man may be disappointed or pained by the result.

May I ask those who have not differed with me to join with me in this same spirit toward those who have? And now let me close by asking three hearty cheers for our brave soldiers and seamen and their gallant and skilful commanders.

Reply to Committee on the Electoral Count

February 9, 1865

[Lincoln had been renominated for the Presidency by the Republican Convention which met in Baltimore on June 7, 1864, and was elected on November 8 by a plurality of nearly half a million in the popular vote. In the Electoral College he had 212 votes to 21 for McClellan.]

WITH deep gratitude to my countrymen for this mark of their confidence ; with a distrust of my own ability to perform the duty required under the most favorable circumstances, and now rendered doubly difficult by existing national perils ; yet with a firm reliance on the strength of our free government, and the eventual loyalty of the people to the just principles upon which it is founded, and above all with an unshaken faith in the Supreme Ruler of nations, I accept this trust. Be pleased to signify this to the respective Houses of Congress.

Second Inaugural Address

March 4, 1865

["The 'Second Inaugural'—a written composition, though read to the citizens from the steps of the Capitol—well illustrates our words. Mr. Lincoln had to tell his countrymen that, after a four years' struggle, the war was practically ended. The four years' agony, the passion of love which he felt for his country, his joy in her salvation, his sense of tenderness for those who fell, of pity mixed with sternness for the men who had deluged the land with blood —all the thoughts these feelings inspired were behind Lincoln pressing for expression. A writer of less power would have been overwhelmed. Lincoln remained master of the emotional and intellectual situation. In three or four hundred words that burn with the heat of their compression, he tells the history of the war and reads its lesson. No nobler thoughts were ever conceived. No man ever found words more adequate to his desire. Here is the whole tale of the nation's shame and misery, of her heroic struggles to free herself therefrom, and of her victory. Had Lincoln written a hundred times as much more, he would not have said more fully what he desired to say. Every thought receives its complete expression, and there is no word employed which does not directly and manifestly contribute to the devel-

Second Inaugural Address

opment of the central thought."—*The (London)* *Spectator*, *May* 2d, 1891.
Compare also Lincoln's letter to Thurlow Weed at the close of this volume of selections.]

Fellow-countrymen : At this second appearing to take the oath of the presidential office, there is less occasion for an extended address than there was at the first. Then a statement, somewhat in detail, of a course to be pursued, seemed fitting and proper. Now, at the expiration of four years, during which public declarations have been constantly called forth on every point and phase of the great contest which still absorbs the attention and engrosses the energies of the nation, little that is new could be presented. The progress of our arms, upon which all else chiefly depends, is as well known to the public as to myself ; and it is, I trust, reasonably satisfactory and encouraging to all. With high hope for the future, no prediction in regard to it is ventured.

On the occasion corresponding to this four years ago, all thoughts were anxiously directed to an impending civil war. All dreaded it—all sought to avert it. While the inaugural address was being delivered from this place, devoted altogether to saving the Union without war, insurgent agents were in the city seeking to destroy it without war—seeking to dissolve the Union, and divide effects, by negotiation. Both parties deprecated war ; but one of them would make war rather than let the nation sur-

Abraham Lincoln

vive ; and the other would accept war rather than let it perish.   And the war came.

One-eighth of the whole population were colored slaves, not distributed generally over the Union, but localized in the Southern part of it. These slaves constituted a peculiar and powerful interest.   All knew that this interest was, somehow, the cause of the war.   To strengthen, perpetuate, and extend this interest was the object for which the insurgents would rend the Union, even by war ; while the government claimed no right to do more than to restrict the territorial enlargement of it.

Neither party expected for the war the magnitude or the duration which it has already attained.   Neither anticipated that the cause of the conflict might cease with, or even before, the conflict itself should cease.   Each looked for an easier triumph, and a result less fundamental and astounding.   Both read the same Bible, and pray to the same God ; and each invokes his aid against the other.   It may seem strange that any men should dare to ask a just God's assistance in wringing their bread from the sweat of other men's faces ; but let us judge not, that we be not judged.   The prayers of both could not be answered—that of neither has been answered fully.

The Almighty has his own purposes.   " Woe unto the world because of offenses ! for it must needs be that offenses come ; but woe to that man by whom the offense cometh."   If we

104

Second Inaugural Address

shall suppose that American slavery is one of those offenses which, in the providence of God, must needs come, but which, having continued through his appointed time, he now wills to remove, and that he gives to both North and South this terrible war, as the woe due to those oy whom the offense came, shall we discern therein any departure from those divine attributes which the believers in a living God always ascribe to him? Fondly do we hope—fervently do we pray—that this mighty scourge of war may speedily pass away. Yet, if God wills that it continue until all the wealth piled by the bondman's two hundred and fifty years of unrequited toil shall be s ınk, and until every drop of blood drawn with the lash shall be paid by another drawn with the sword, as was said three thousand years ago, so still it must be said, " The judgments of the Lord are true and righteous altogether."

With malice toward none ; with charity for all ; with firmness in the right, as God gives us to see the right, let us strive on to finish the work we are in ; to bind up the nation's wounds ; to care for him who shall have borne the battle, and for his widow, and his orphan—to do all which may achieve and cherish a just and lasting peace among ourselves, and with all nations.

Letters

107

To McClellan

February 3, 1862

[General McClellan had succeeded General Scott on November 1, 1861, as •Commander-in-Chief (under the President) of all the armies of the United States. On January 31, 1862, the President had issued his " Special War Order No. 1," directing a forward movement of the Army of the Potomac. This order conflicted with plans which McClellan had formed, and he remonstrated. Lincoln's reply is a good illustration of his power of compact statement, as well as of his mastery of the military situation.]

Executive Mansion, Washington, February 3, 1862.

MAJOR-GENERAL MCCLELLAN :

MY DEAR SIR : You and I have distinct and different plans for a movement of the Army of the Potomac—yours to be down the Chesapeake, up the Rappahannock to Urbana, and across land to the terminus of the railroad on the York River ; mine to move directly to a point on the railroad southwest of Manassas.

If you will give me satisfactory answers to the following questions, I shall gladly yield my plan to yours.

First. Does not your plan involve a greatly

larger expenditure of time and money than mine?

Second. Wherein is a victory more certain by your plan than mine?

Third. Wherein is a victory more valuable by your plan than mine?

Fourth. In fact, would it not be less valuable in this, that it would break no great line of the enemy's communications, while mine would?

Fifth. In case of disaster, would not a retreat be more difficult by your plan than mine?

Yours truly,

ABRAHAM LINCOLN.

MAJOR-GENERAL McCLELLAN.

To Seward

June 28, 1862

[This letter was written to W. H. Seward, the Secretary of State, shortly after the Union victories in Kentucky and Tennessee and upon the Mississippi River, in the spring of 1862.]

Executive Mansion, June 28, 1862.

HON. W. H. SEWARD :

MY DEAR SIR : My view of the present condition of the war is about as follows :

The evacuation of Corinth and our delay by the flood in the Chickahominy have enabled the enemy to concentrate too much force in Richmond for McClellan to successfully attack. In fact there soon will be no substantial rebel force anywhere else. But if we send all the force from here to McClellan, the enemy will, before we can know of it, send a force from Richmond and take Washington. Or if a large part of the western army be brought here to McClellan, they will let us have Richmond, and retake Tennessee, Kentucky, Missouri, etc. What should be done is to hold what we have in the West, open the Mississippi, and take Chattanooga and East Tennessee without more. A reasonable force should in every event be

Abraham Lincoln

kept about Washington for its protection.
Then let the country give us a hundred thousand new troops in the shortest possible time,
which, added to McClellan directly or indirectly,
will take Richmond without endangering any
other place which we now hold, and will substantially end the war. I expect to maintain
this contest until successful, or till I die, or am
conquered, or my term expires, or Congress or
the country forsake me ; and I would publicly
appeal to the country for this new force were
it not that I fear a general panic and stampede
would follow, so hard it is to have a thing understood as it really is. I think the new force
should be all, or nearly all, infantry, principally
because such can be raised most cheaply and
quickly.

Yours very truly,

A. LINCOLN.

To Greeley

August 22, 1862

[Horace Greeley, the famous editor of the New York *Tribune*, though an ardent opponent of slavery, was a constant critic of Lincoln's policy, and indeed opposed his renomination for the Presidency. His erratic editorials concerning the Administration were a continual source of anxiety to Lincoln.]

Executive Mansion, Washington, August 22, 1862.

HON. HORACE GREELEY :

DEAR SIR : I have just read yours of the 19th, addressed to myself through the New York *Tribune*. If there be in it any statements or assumptions of fact which I may know to be erroneous, I do not, now and here, controvert them. If there be in it any inferences which I may believe to be falsely drawn, I do not, now and here, argue against them. If there be perceptible in it an impatient and dictatorial tone, I waive it in deference to an old friend whose heart I have always supposed to be right.

As to the policy I " seem to be pursuing," as you say, I have not meant to leave any one in doubt.

I would save the Union. I would save it the shortest way under the Constitution. The sooner the national authority can be restored, the nearer the Union will be " the Union as it was." If there be those who would not save the Union unless they could at the same time save slavery, I do not agree with them. If there be those who would not save the Union unless they could at the same time destroy slavery, I do not agree with them. My paramount object in this struggle is to save the Union, and is not either to save or to destroy slavery. If I could save the Union without freeing any slave, I would do it ; and if I could save it by freeing all the slaves, I would do it ; and if I could save it by freeing some and leaving others alone, I would also do that. What I do about slavery and the colored race, I do because I believe it helps to save the Union ; and what I forbear, I forbear because I do not believe it would help to save the Union. I shall do less whenever I shall believe what I am doing hurts the cause, and I shall do more whenever I shall believe doing more will help the cause. I shall try to correct errors when shown to be errors, and I shall adopt new views so fast as they shall appear to be true views.

I have here stated my purpose according to my view of official duty ; and I intend no modification of my oft-expressed personal wish that all men everywhere could be free.

Yours,

A. LINCOLN.

To the Workingmen of Manchester

January 19, 1863

[The blockade of Confederate ports during the war was naturally a severe blow to the English manufacturing centres like Manchester, which had depended upon the Southern States for their supply of cotton. But the working classes of England, in marked contrast with the upper classes, displayed strong Union sympathies throughout the struggle. An address from the Manchester workingmen called forth this admirable reply from the President.]

Executive Mansion, Washington, January 19, 1863.

TO THE WORKINGMEN OF MANCHESTER : I have the honor to acknowledge the receipt of the address and resolutions which you sent me on the eve of the new year. When I came, on the 4th of March, 1861, through a free and constitutional election to preside in the Government of the United States, the country was found at the verge of civil war. Whatever might have been the cause, or whosesoever the fault, one duty, paramount to all others, was before me, namely, to maintain and preserve at once the Constitution and the integrity of the Federal Republic. A conscientious purpose to perform this duty is the key to all the measures of administration which have been and to all which will hereafter be pursued. Under our frame of government

and my official oath, I could not depart from
this purpose if I would. It is not always in the
power of governments to enlarge or restrict the
scope of moral results which follow the policies
that they may deem it necessary for the public
safety from time to time to adopt.

I have understood well that the duty of self-
preservation rests solely with the American people ; but I have at the same time been aware
that favor or disfavor of foreign nations might
have a material influence in enlarging or pro-
longing the struggle with disloyal men in which
the country is engaged. A fair examination of
history has served to authorize a belief that the
past actions and influences of the United States
were generally regarded as having been bene-
ficial toward mankind. I have, therefore, reck-
oned upon the forbearance of nations. Circumstances—to some of which you kindly allude—
induce me especially to expect that if justice
and good faith should be practised by the
United States, they would encounter no hostile
influence on the part of Great Britain. It is
now a pleasant duty to acknowledge the dem-
onstration you have given of your desire that a
spirit of amity and peace toward this country
may prevail in the councils of your Queen, who
is respected and esteemed in your own country
only more than she is by the kindred nation
which has its home on this side of the Atlantic.

I know and deeply deplore the sufferings
which the workingmen at Manchester, and in

To Workingmen of Manchester

all Europe, are called to endure in this crisis.
It has been often and studiously represented
that the attempt to overthrow this government,
which was built upon the foundation of human
rights, and to substitute for it one which should
rest exclusively on the basis of human slavery,
was likely to obtain the favor of Europe.
Through the action of our disloyal citizens, the
workingmen of Europe have been subjected to
severe trials, for the purpose of forcing their
sanction to that attempt. Under the circumstances, I cannot but regard your decisive utterances upon the question as an instance of
sublime Christian heroism which has not been
surpassed in any age or in any country. It is
indeed an energetic and reinspiring assurance
of the inherent power of truth, and of the ultimate and universal triumph of justice, humanity, and freedom. I do not doubt that the sentiments you have expressed will be sustained
by your great nation ; and, on the other hand,
I have no hesitation in assuring you that they
will excite admiration, esteem, and the most re-
ciprocal feelings of friendship among the American people. I hail this interchange of sentiment, therefore, as an augury that whatever
else may happen, whatever misfortune may be-
fall your country or my own, the peace and
friendship which now exist between the two
nations will be, as it shall be my desire to make
them, perpetual.

ABRAHAM LINCOLN.

To Hooker

[This letter to General Joseph Hooker, appointing him the successor of General Burnside as commander of the Army of the Potomac, is one of Lincoln's most characteristic utterances —frank, kind, and gravely ironical. Notice the phrase, " I will risk the dictatorship."]

Executive Mansion, Washington, January 26, 1863.

MAJOR-GENERAL HOOKER :

GENERAL : I have placed you at the head of the Army of the Potomac. Of course I have done this upon what appear to me to be sufficient reasons, and yet I think it best for you to know that there are some things in regard to which I am not quite satisfied with you. I believe you to be a brave and skilful soldier, which of course I like. I also believe you do not mix politics with your profession, in which you are right. You have confidence in yourself, which is a valuable if not an indispensable quality. You are ambitious, which, within reasonable bounds, does good rather than harm ; but I think that during General Burnside's command of the army you have taken counsel of your ambition and thwarted him as much as you could, in which you did a great wrong to

118

the country and to a most meritorious and honorable brother officer. I have heard, in such a way as to believe it, of your recently saying that both the army and the government needed a dictator. Of course it was not for this, but in spite of it, that I have given you the command. Only those generals who gain successes can set up dictators. What I now ask of you is military success, and I will risk the dictatorship. The government will support you to the utmost of its ability, which is neither more nor less than it has done and will do for all commanders. I much fear that the spirit which you have aided to infuse into the army, of criticising their commander and withholding confidence from him, will now turn upon you. I shall assist you as far as I can to put it down. Neither you nor Napoleon, if he were alive again, could get any good out of an army while such a spirit prevails in it ; and now beware of rashness. Beware of rashness, but with energy and sleepless vigilance go forward and give us victories.

Yours very truly,

A. LINCOLN.

To Burnside

July 27, 1863

[This telegram is noticeable for its brief but comprehensive description of General Grant.]

War Department, Washington, July 27, 1863.

MAJOR-GENERAL BURNSIDE, Cincinnati, Ohio :

Let me explain. In General Grant's first despatch after the fall of Vicksburg, he said, among other things, he would send the Ninth Corps to you. Thinking it would be pleasant to you, I asked the Secretary of War to telegraph you the news. For some reasons never mentioned to us by General Grant, they have not been sent, though we have seen outside intimations that they took part in the expedition against Jackson. General Grant is a copious worker and fighter, but a very meager writer or telegrapher. No doubt he changed his purpose in regard to the Ninth Corps for some sufficient reason, but has forgotten to notify us of it.

A. LINCOLN.

To Edward Everett

November 20, 1863

[See the note prefixed to Lincoln's Gettysburg address.]

Executive Mansion, Washington, November 20, 1863.

HON. EDWARD EVERETT :

MY DEAR SIR : Your kind note of to-day is received. In our respective parts yesterday, you could not have been excused to make a short address, nor I a long one. I am pleased to know that, in your judgment, the little I did say was not entirely a failure. Of course I knew Mr. Everett would not fail, and yet, while the whole discourse was eminently satisfactory, and will be of great value, there were passages in it which transcended my expectations. The point made against the theory of the General Government being only an agency whose principals are the States, was new to me, and, as I think, is one of the best arguments for the national supremacy. The tribute to our noble women for their angel ministering to the suffering soldiers surpasses in its way, as do the subjects of it, whatever has gone before.

Our sick boy, for whom you kindly inquire, we hope is past the worst.

Your obedient servant,

A. LINCOLN.

To Grant

April 30, 1864

[The spring campaign of 1864 marked " the beginning of the end" of the Rebellion. This letter is one of many proofs of Lincoln's absolute confidence in Grant's generalship.]

Executive Mansion, Washington, April 30, 1864.

LIEUTENANT-GENERAL GRANT :

Not expecting to see you again before the spring campaign opens, I wish to express in this way my entire satisfaction with what you have done up to this time, so far as I understand it. The particulars of your plans I neither know nor seek to know. You are vigilant and self-reliant ; and, pleased with this, I wish not to obtrude any constraints or restraints upon you. While I am very anxious that any great disaster or capture of our men in great numbers shall be avoided, I know these points are less likely to escape your attention than they would be mine. If there is anything wanting which is within my power to give, do not fail to let me know it. And now, with a brave army and a just cause, may God sustain you.

Yours very truly,

A. LINCOLN.

To Mrs. Bixby

November 21, 1864

Executive Mansion, Washington, November 21, 1864.

MRS. BIXBY, Boston, Massachusetts :

DEAR MADAM : I have been shown in the files of the War Department a statement of the Adjutant-General of Massachusetts that you are the mother of five sons who have died gloriously on the field of battle. I feel how weak and fruitless must be any words of mine which should attempt to beguile you from the grief of a loss so overwhelming. But I cannot refrain from tendering to you the consolation that may be found in the thanks of the Republic they died to save. I pray that our heavenly Father may assuage the anguish of your bereavement, and leave you only the cherished memory of the loved and lost, and the solemn pride that must be yours to have laid so costly a sacrifice upon the altar of freedom.

Yours very sincerely and respectfully,

ABRAHAM LINCOLN.

To Thurlow Weed

March 15, 1865

[This most interesting letter, written a month before Lincoln's assassination, should be read in connection with the second inaugural address.]

Executive Mansion, Washington, March 15, 1865.

DEAR MR. WEED :

Every one likes a compliment. Thank you for yours on my little notification speech and on the recent inaugural address. I expect the latter to wear as well as—perhaps better than—anything I have produced ; but I believe it is not immediately popular. Men are not flattered by being shown that there has been a difference of purpose between the Almighty and them. To deny it, however, in this case, is to deny that there is a God governing the world. It is a truth which I thought needed to be told, and, as whatever of humiliation there is in it falls most directly on myself, I thought others might afford for me to tell it.

Truly yours,

A. LINCOLN.

Appendix

"Lincoln's Lost Speech"*

THE Republican party was first organized in Illinois on May 29th, 1856, at a State convention held in Bloomington. It was here that Abraham Lincoln made the speech which definitely severed his relations with the Whigs and allied him to the new organization. For two years previous he had been slowly working toward this change. The failure of his political ambitions in the summer of 1849 had decided him henceforth to devote himself to the law. For nearly six years he had kept this resolution. Then, in the spring of 1854, the passage by Congress of the Kansas-Nebraska bill repealing the Missouri Compromise of 1820, and establishing the principle of popular sovereignty, had so aroused him that he flung himself again into politics.

Elected to the legislature in the fall of 1854, Lincoln had resigned in order to contest the vacant seat in the United States Senate. He showed in this campaign how much more important he considered it to insure legislation against slavery extension than to elect one of his own party ; for when he found that the bal-

* Copyright. 1896, by Sarah A. Whitney.

127

ance of power in the legislature which was to elect the senator was held by five anti-Nebraska Democrats, he persuaded his supporters to go over to the five, whom he knew to be of the same mind as himself in regard to the extension of slavery, rather than to allow a combination on a man who would oppose the measure but lukewarmly.

When, in the spring of 1856, the Illinois opponents of slavery extension had sufficient strength to form another branch of the now rapidly growing Republican party, Lincoln was ready to join them. The speech he made at the first convention was long known in Illinois as " Lincoln's Lost Speech," a name given it because the reporters were so carried away by his eloquence that they forgot to take notes and could give no report to their papers. As Lincoln himself refused to try to write it out, it was supposed to have been, in fact, a " lost speech."

It seems, however, that though the reporters, under the effect of Lincoln's eloquence, all lost their heads, there was at least one auditor who had enough control to pursue his usual habit of making notes of the speeches he heard. This was a young lawyer on the same circuit as Lincoln, Mr. H. C. Whitney. For some three weeks before the convention, Lincoln and Whitney had been attending court at Danv'lle. They had discussed the political situation in the State carefully, and to Whitney, Lincoln had

" Lincoln's Lost Speech "

stated his convictions and determinations.
Knowing as he did that Lincoln had not written out his speech, Whitney went to the convention intending to take notes.   Fortunately,
he had a cool enough head to keep to his purpose.   These notes Whitney kept for many
years, always intending to write them out, but
never attending to it, until in 1896 *McClure's
Magazine* learned that he had them, and persuaded him to carry out his intention.   Mr.
Whitney does not claim that he has made a perfect report.   He does claim, however, that the
argument is correct, and that in many cases the
expressions are exact.

The speech has been submitted to several of
those who were at the Bloomington convention,
among others to Mr. Joseph Medill, editor of
the *Chicago Tribune*, who says :

Mr. Medill's Letter

(*Slightly condensed*)

Chicago, May 15, 1896.

EDITOR McCLURE'S MAGAZINE,
     NEW YORK CITY :

DEAR SIR : You invited my attention recently
to H. C. Whitney's report of the great radical
" anti-Nebraska" speech of Mr. Lincoln, delivered in Bloomington, May 29th, 1856, before
the first Republican State Convention of Illinois ;
and, as I was present as a delegate and heard
it, you ask me to state how accurately, accord-

ing to my best recollection, it is reproduced in this report.

I have carefully and reflectively read it, and taking into account that Mr. Whitney did not take down the speech stenographically, but only took notes, and afterward wrote them out in full, he has reproduced with remarkable accuracy what Mr. Lincoln said, largely in his identical language and partly in synonymous terms. The report is close enough in thought and word to recall the wonderful speech delivered forty years ago with vivid freshness. No one was expecting a great speech at the time. We all knew that he could say something worthy of the occasion, but nobody anticipated such a Demosthenean outburst of oratory. There was great political excitement at the time in Illinois and all over the old Northwest, growing out of the efforts of the South to introduce slavery into Kansas and Nebraska. The free-soil men were highly wrought up in opposition, and Mr. Lincoln partook of their feelings.

I am unable to point out those sentences and parts of the reported speech which vary most in phraseology from the precise language he used, because there is an approximation of his words in every part of it. The ideas uttered are all there. The sequence of argument is accurately given. The invectives hurled at pro-slavery aggression are not exaggerated in the report of the speech. Some portions of the argument citing pro-slavery aggressions seem rather more

"Lincoln's Lost Speech"

elaborate than he delivered ; but he was speaking under a high degree of excitement, and the
convention was in a responsive mood, and it is
impossible to be certain about it. The least
that can be said is, that the Whitney report,
not being shorthand, is yet a remarkably good
one, and is the only one in existence that repro-
duces the speech.

During all the preceding year the public mind
of the West had been lashed into a high state
of commotion over the repeal of the Missouri
Compromise the year before, which had excluded the introduction of slavery into all territory north of 36.30 degrees. Taking advantage
of the repeal, the slaveholders of Missouri and
other slave States, aided by the administration
of Franklin Pierce, were striving to convert
Kansas and Nebraska into slave States. This
bad work was carried on actively in the spring
of 1856. Many houses of the free-State men of
the new city of Lawrence, including their hotel,
were burnt. Printing-offices were destroyed ;
store goods were carried off ; horses and cattle
were stolen ; sharp fights were taking place ;
men were being killed, and civil war was rag-
ing in " bleeding Kansas."

While this state of things was going on, the
first State Republican Convention ever held in
Illinois assembled in Bloomington, May 29th,
1856. It was composed of Abolitionists, Free-
Soil Whigs, and " Anti-Nebraska" Democrats.
Owen Lovejoy embodied the first named, Abra-

ham Lincoln and John M. Palmer, the second and third elements ; the whole united, made the new Republican party.

At this Bloomington Republican convention delegates were appointed who voted to nominate Frémont for President. Abraham Lincoln was placed at the head of the State electoral ticket, and Colonel Bissell (of the Mexican War) was nominated for Governor, and free-soil resolutions were passed. Mr. John M. Palmer presided and made a stirring free-soil speech.

Mr. Emery, a "free-State" man just from "bleeding Kansas," told of the "border ruffian" raids from Missouri upon the free-State settlers in Kansas : the burnings, robberies, and murders they were then committing ; and asked for help to repel them. When he finished, Lincoln was vociferously called for from all parts of Major's large hall. He came forward and took the platform beside the presiding officer. At first his voice was shrill and hesitating. There was a curious introspective look in his eyes, which lasted for a few moments. Then his voice began to move steadily and smoothly forward, and the modulations were under perfect control from thenceforward to the finish. He warmed up as he went on, and spoke more rapidly ; he looked a foot taller as he straightened himself to his full height, and his eyes flashed fire ; his countenance became wrapped in intense emotion ; he rushed along like a thunderstorm. He prophesied war as the outcome of

these aggressions, and poured forth hot denunciations upon the slave power. The convention
was kept in an uproar, applauding and cheering and stamping; and this reacted on the
speaker, and gave him a tongue of fire. The
thrilling scene in that old Bloomington hall
forty years ago arises in my mind as vividly as
the day after its enactment.

There stood Lincoln in the forefront, erect,
tall, and majestic in appearance, hurling thun-
derbolts at the foes of freedom, while the great
convention roared its endorsement! I never
witnessed such a scene before or since. As he
described the aims and aggressions of the un-
appeasable slaveholders and the servility of
their Northern allies as illustrated by the per-
fidious repeal of the Missouri Compromise two
years previously, and their grasping after the
rich prairies of Kansas and Nebraska, to blight
them with slavery and to deprive free labor of
this rich inheritance, and exhorted the friends
of freedom to resist them to the death, the convention went fairly wild. It paralleled or ex-
ceeded the scene in the Revolutionary Virginia
convention of eighty-one years before, when
Patrick Henry invoked death if liberty could
not be preserved, and said, "After all we must
fight." Strange, too, that this same man received death a few years afterward while con-
ferring freedom on the slave race and preserv-
ing the American Union from dismemberment.

While Mr. Lincoln did not write out even a

memorandum of his Bloomington speech beforehand, neither was it extemporary. He intended days before to make it, and conned it over
in his mind in outline, and gathered his facts,
and arranged his arguments in regular order,
and trusted to the inspiration of the occasion to
furnish him the diction with which to clothe the
skeleton of his great oration. It is difficult to
name any speech by another orator delivered
on the same subject about that time or subsequently that equalled it—not excepting those
made by Sumner, Seward, or Chase—in strength
of argument or dramatic power.

It was my journalistic duty, though a delegate to the convention, to make a longhand report of the speeches delivered, for the Chicago
Tribune. I did make a few paragraphs of report of what Lincoln said in the first eight or
ten minutes ; but I became so absorbed in his
magnetic oratory that I forgot myself and
ceased to take notes, and joined with the convention in cheering and stamping and clapping
to the end of his speech. I well remember that
after Lincoln had sat down and calm had succeeded the tempest, I waked out of a sort of
hypnotic trance, and then thought of my report
for the *Tribune.* There was nothing written
but an abbreviated introduction. It was some
sort of satisfaction to find that I had not been
"scooped," as all the newspaper men present had been equally carried away by the
excitement caused by the wonderful oration,

"Lincoln's Lost Speech"

and had made no report or sketch of the speech.

It was fortunate, however, that a cool-nerved young lawyer and ardent friend of Lincoln's who was present, with nimble fingers took down so much of the exact words as they fell from the great orator's lips, that he was afterward able to reproduce the speech almost identically as it was uttered, and has thus saved it to posterity.

Mr. Lincoln was strongly urged by party friends to write out his speech, to be used as a campaign document for the Frémont Presidential contest of that year ; but he declared that "it would be impossible for him to recall the language he used on that occasion, as he had spoken under some excitement."

My belief is that, after Mr. Lincoln cooled down, he was rather pleased that his speech had not been reported, as it was too radical in expression on the slavery question for the digestion of central and southern Illinois at that time, and that he preferred to let it stand as a remembrance in the minds of his audience. But be that as it may, the effect of it was such on his hearers that he bounded to the leadership of the new Republican party of Illinois, and no man afterward ever thought of disputing that position with him. On that occasion he planted the seed which germinated into a Presidential candidacy, and that gave him the nomination over Seward at the Chicago Convention of 1860.

Abraham Lincoln

which placed him in the Presidential chair, there to complete his predestined work of destroying slavery and making freedom universal, but yielding his life as a sacrifice for the glorious deeds.

I am, very respectfully yours,

JOSEPH MEDILL.

Mr. Lincoln's Speech

Mr. Chairman and Gentlemen : I was over at [cries of " Platform !"   " Take the platform !"]—I say, that while I was at Danville Court, some of our friends of anti-Nebraska got together in Springfield and elected me as one delegate to represent old Sangamon with them in this convention, and I am here certainly as a sympathizer in this movement and by virtue of that meeting and selection.   But we can hardly be called delegates strictly, inasmuch as, properly speaking, we represent nobody but ourselves.   I think it altogether fair to say that we have no anti-Nebraska party in Sangamon, although there is a good deal of anti-Nebraska feeling there ; but I say for myself, and I think I may speak also for my colleagues, that we who are here fully approve of the platform and of all that has been done [a voice : " Yes !"] ; and even if we are not regularly delegates, it will be right for me to answer your call to speak.   I suppose we truly stand for the public sentiment of Sangamon on the great question

136

of the repeal, although we do not yet represent many numbers who have taken a distinct position on the question.

We are in a trying time—it ranges above mere party—and this movement to call a halt and turn our steps backward needs all the help and good counsels it can get ; for unless popular opinion makes itself very strongly felt, and a change is made in our present course, *blood will flow on account of Nebraska, and brother's hand will be raised against brother !* [The last sentence was uttered in such an earnest, impressive, if not, indeed, tragic, manner, as to make a cold chill creep over me. Others gave a similar experience.]

I have listened with great interest to the earnest appeal made to Illinois men by the gentleman from Lawrence [James S. Emery] who has just addressed us so eloquently and forcibly. I was deeply moved by his statement of the wrongs done to free-State men out there. I think it just to say that all true men North should sympathize with them, and ought to be willing to do any possible and needful thing to right their wrongs. But we must not promise what we ought not, lest we be called on to perform what we cannot ; we must be calm and moderate, and consider the whole difficulty, and determine what is possible and just. We must not be led by excitement and passion to do that which our sober judgments would not approve in our cooler moments. We have

higher aims ; we will have more serious business than to dally with temporary measures.

We are here to stand firmly for a principle—
to stand firmly for a right. We know that
great political and moral wrongs are done, and
outrages committed, and we denounce those
wrongs and outrages, although we cannot, at
present, do much more. But we desire to reach
out beyond those personal outrages and establish a rule that will apply to all, and so prevent
any future outrages.

We have seen to-day that every shade of
popular opinion is represented here, with *Freedom* or rather *Free-Soil* as the basis. We have
come together as in some sort representatives
of popular opinion against the extension of
slavery into territory now free in fact as well
as by law, and the pledged word of the statesmen of the nation who are now no more. We
come—we are here assembled together—to protest as well as we can against a great wrong,
and to take measures, as well as we now can,
to make that wrong right ; to place the nation,
as far as it may be possible now, as it was before the repeal of the Missouri Compromise ;
and the plain way to do this is to restore the
Compromise, and to demand and determine
that *Kansas shall be free !* [Immense applause.] While we affirm, and reaffirm, if necessary, our devotion to the principles of the
Declaration of Independence, let our practical
work here be limited to the above. We know

that there is not a perfect agreement of sentiment here on the public questions which might
be rightfully considered in this convention, and
that the indignation which we all must feel cannot be helped ; but all of us must give up something for the good of the cause.   There is one
desire which is uppermost in the mind, one
wish common to us all—to which no dissent
will be made ; and I counsel you earnestly to
bury all resentment, to sink all personal feeling, make all things work to a common purpose
in which we are united and agreed about, and
which all present will agree is absolutely necessary—which *must* be done by any rightful
mode if there be such : *Slavery must be kept
out of Kansas !* [Applause.]   The test—the
pinch—is right there.   If we lose Kansas to
freedom, an example will be set which will
prove fatal to freedom in the end.   We, therefore, in the language of the *Bible*, must " lay
the axe to the root of the tree."   Temporizing
will not do longer ; now is the time for decision
—for firm, persistent, resolute action.   [Ap-
plause.]

The Nebraska bill, or rather Nebraska law,
is not one of wholesome legislation, but was
and is an act of legislative usurpation, whose
result, if not indeed intention, is to make slavery
national ; and unless headed off in some effec-
tive way, we are in a fair way to see this land
of boasted freedom converted into a land of
slavery in fact.   [Sensation.]   Just open your

two eyes, and see if this be not so. I need do
no more than state, to command universal approval, that almost the entire North, as well as
a large following in the border States, is radi-
cally opposed to the planting of slavery in free
territory. Probably in a popular vote throughout the nation nine-tenths of the voters in the
free States, and at least one-half in the border
States, if they could express their sentiments
freely, would vote NO on such an issue ; and it
is safe to say that two-thirds of the votes of the
entire nation would be opposed to it. And yet,
in spite of this overbalancing of sentiment in
this free country, we are in a fair way to see
Kansas present itself for admission as a slave
State. Indeed, it is a felony, by the local law
of Kansas, to deny that slavery exists there
even now. By every principle of law, a negro
in Kansas is free ; yet the *bogus* legislature
makes it an infamous crime to tell him that he
is free !*

The party lash and the fear of ridicule will

---

* Statutes of Kansas, 1855, Chapter 151, Section 12. If
any free person, by speaking or by writing, assert or
maintain that persons have not the right to hold slaves
in this Territory, or shall introduce into this Territory,
print, publish, write, circulate . . . any book, paper,
magazine, pamphlet, or circular containing any denial
of the right of persons to hold slaves in this Territory,
such person shall be deemed guilty of *felony*, and pun-
ished by imprisonment at hard labor for a term of not
less than two years.

Sec. 13. No person who is conscientiously opposed to
holding slaves, or who does not admit the right to
hold slaves in this Territory, shall sit as a juror on the
trial of any prosecution for any violation of any sections of this Act.

"Lincoln's Lost Speech"

overawe justice and liberty ; for it is a singular
fact, but none the less a fact, and well known
by the most common experience, that men will
do things under the terror of the party lash that
they would not on any account or for any consideration do otherwise ; while men who will
march up to the mouth of a loaded cannon without shrinking, will run from the terrible name
of "Abolitionist," even when pronounced by a
worthless creature whom they, with good reason, despise.   For instance—to press this point
a little—Judge Douglas introduced his anti-
Nebraska bill in January ; and we had an ex-
tra session of our legislature in the succeeding
February, in which were seventy-five Democrats ; and at a party caucus, fully attended,
there were just three votes out of the whole
seventy-five, for the measure.   But in a few
days orders came on from Washington, com-
manding them to approve the measure ; the
party lash was applied, and it was brought up
again in caucus, and passed by a large majority.   The masses were against it, but party
necessity carried it ; and it was passed through
the lower house of Congress against the will of
the people, for the same reason.   Here is where
the greatest danger lies—that, while we profess
to be a government of law and reason, law will
give way to violence on demand of this awful
and crushing power.   Like the great Jugger-
naut—I think that is the name—the great idol,
it crushes everything that comes in its way, and

makes a—or as I read once, in a black-letter law book, "a slave is a human being who is legally not a *person*, but a *thing*." And if the safeguards to liberty are broken down, as is now attempted, when they have made *things* of all the free negroes, how long, think you, before they will begin to make *things* of poor white men ? [Applause.] Be not deceived. Revolutions do not go backward. The founder of the Democratic party declared that *all* men were created equal. His successor in the leadership has written the word "white" before men, making it read " all *white* men are created equal." Pray, will or may not the Knownothings, if they should get in power, add the word " protestant," making it read " *all protestant white men*" ?

Meanwhile the hapless negro is the fruitful subject of reprisals in other quarters. John Pettit, whom Tom Benton paid his respects to, you will recollect, calls the immortal Declaration " a self-evident lie ;" while at the birthplace of freedom—in the shadow of Bunker Hill and of the " cradle of liberty," at the home of the Adamses and Warren and Otis—Choate, from our side of the house, dares to fritter away the birthday promise of liberty by proclaiming the Declaration to be " a string of glittering generalities ;" and the Southern Whigs, working hand in hand with pro-slavery Democrats, are making Choate's theories practical. Thomas Jefferson, a slaveholder, mindful of the moral

" Lincoln's Lost Speech "

element in slavery, solemnly declared that he
" trembled for his country when he remembered that God is just ;" while Judge Douglas,
with an insignificant wave of the hand, " don't
care whether slavery is voted up or voted
down." Now, if slavery is right, or even negative, he has a right to treat it in this trifling
manner. But if it is a moral and political
wrong, as all Christendom considers it to be,
how can he answer to God for this attempt to
spread and fortify it ? [Applause.]

But no man, and Judge Douglas no more
than any other, can maintain a negative, or
merely neutral, position on this question ; and,
accordingly, he avows that the Union was made
by white men and *for* white men and their descendants. As matter of fact, the first branch
of the proposition is historically true ; the government was made by white men, and they
were and are the superior race. This I admit.
But the corner-stone of the government, so to
speak, was the declaration that " *all* men are
created equal," and all entitled to " life, liberty,
and the pursuit of happiness." [Applause.]

And not only so, but the framers of the Constitution were particular to keep out of that instrument the word " slave," the reason being
that slavery would ultimately come to an end,
and they did not wish to have any reminder
that in this free country human beings were
ever prostituted to slavery. [Applause.] Nor
is it any argument that we are superior and the

143

negro inferior—that he has but one talent while we have ten. Let the negro possess the little he has in independence ; if he has but one talent, he should be permitted to keep the little he has. [Applause.] But slavery will endure no test of reason or logic ; and yet its advocates, like Douglas, use a sort of bastard logic, or noisy assumption, it might better be termed, like the above, in order to prepare the mind for the gradual, but none the less certain, encroachments of the Moloch of slavery upon the fair domain of freedom. But however much you may argue upon it, or smother it in soft phrases, slavery can only be maintained by force—by violence. The repeal of the Missouri Compromise was by violence. It was a violation of both law and the sacred obligations of honor, to overthrow and trample underfoot a solemn compromise, obtained by the fearful loss to freedom of one of the fairest of our Western domains. Congress violated the will and confidence of its constituents in voting for the bill ; and while public sentiment, as shown by the elections of 1854, demanded the restoration of this compromise, Congress violated its trust by refusing, simply because it had the force of numbers to hold on to it. And murderous violence is being used now, in order to force slavery on to Kansas ; for it cannot be done in any other way. [Se sation.]

The necessary result was to establish the rule of violence—force, instead of the rule of law and reason ; to perpetuate and spread slavery, and, in time, to make it general. We see it at both ends of the line. In Washington, on the very spot where the outrage was started, the fearless Sumner is beaten to insensibility, and is now slowly dying ; while senators who claim to be gentlemen and Christians stood by, countenancing the act, and even applauding it afterward in their places in the Senate. Even Douglas, our man, saw it all and was within helping distance, yet let the murderous blows fall unopposed. Then, at the other end of the line, at the very time Sumner was being murdered, Lawrence was being destroyed for the crime of Freedom. It was the most prominent stronghold of liberty in Kansas, and must give way to the all-dominating power of slavery. Only two days ago, Judge Trumbull found it necessary to propose a bill in the Senate to prevent a general civil war and to restore peace in Kansas.

We live in the midst of alarms ; anxiety beclouds the future ; we expect some new disaster with each newspaper we read. Are we in a healthful political state ? Are not the tendencies plain ? Do not the signs of the times point plainly the way in which we are going ? Sensation.]

In the early days of the Constitution slavery was recognized, by South and North alike, as an evil, and the division of sentiment about it was not controlled by geographical lines or considerations of climate, but by moral and philan-thropic views. Petitions for the abolition of slavery were presented to the very first Con-gress by Virginia and Massachusetts alike. To show the harmony which prevailed, I will state that a fugitive slave law was passed in 1793, with no dissenting voice in the Senate, and but seven dissenting votes in the House. It was, however, a wise law, moderate, and, under the Constitution, a just one. Twenty-five years later, a more stringent law was proposed and defeated ; and thirty-five years after that, the present law, drafted by Mason of Virginia, was passed by Northern votes. I am not, just now, complaining of this law, but I am trying to show how the current sets ; for the proposed law of 1817 was far less offensive than the pres-ent one. In 1774 the Continental Congress pledged itself, without a dissenting vote, to wholly discontinue the slave trade, and to neither purchase nor import any slave ; and less than three months before the passage of the Declaration of Independence, the same Congress which adopted that declaration unani-mously resolved "that *no slave be imported into any of the thirteen United Colonies.*" [Great applause.]

On the second day of July, 1776, the draft of a Declaration of Independence was reported to Congress by the committee, and in it the slave trade was characterized as " an execrable com-merce," as " a piratical warfare," as the " op-

" Lincoln's Lost Speech "

probrium of infidel powers," and as " a cruel war against human nature." [Applause.] All agreed on this except South Carolina and Georgia, and in order to preserve harmony, and from the necessity of the case, these expressions were omitted. Indeed, abolition societies existed as far south as Virginia ; and it is a well-known fact that Washington, Jefferson, Madison, Lee, Henry, Mason, and Pendleton were qualified abolitionists, and much more radical on that subject than we of the Whig and Democratic parties claim to be to-day. On March 1, 1784, Virginia ceded to the confederation all its lands lying northwest of the Ohio River. Jefferson, Chase of Maryland, and Howell of Rhode Island, as a committee on that and territory thereafter *to be ceded*, reported that no slavery should exist after the year 1800. Had this report been adopted, not only the Northwest, but Kentucky, Tennessee, Alabama, and Mississippi also would have been free ; but it required the assent of nine States to ratify it. North Carolina was divided, and thus its vote was lost ; and Delaware, Georgia, and New Jersey refused to vote. In point of fact, as it was, it was assented to by six States. Three years later, on a square vote to exclude slavery from the Northwest, only one vote, and that from New York, was against it. And yet, thirty-seven years later, five thousand citizens of Illinois out of a voting mass of less than twelve thousand, deliberately, after a long and

147

heated contest, voted to introduce slavery in
Illinois ; and, to-day, a large party in the free
State of Illinois are willing to vote to fasten the
shackles of slavery on the fair domain of Kansas, notwithstanding it received the dowry of
freedom long before its birth as a political community.   I repeat, therefore, the question, Is it
not plain in what direction we are tending ?
[Sensation.]   In the colonial time, Mason,
Pendleton, and Jefferson were as hostile to
slavery in Virginia as Otis, Ames, and the
Adamses were in Massachusetts ; and Virginia
made as earnest an effort to get rid of it as old
Massachusetts did.   But circumstances were
against them and they failed ; but not that the
good will of its leading men was lacking.   Yet
within less than fifty years Virginia changed its
tune, and made negro-breeding for the cotton
and sugar States one of its leading industries.
[Laughter and applause.]

In the Constitutional Convention, George
Mason of Virginia made a more violent abolition speech than my friends Lovejoy or Cod-
ding would desire to make here to-day—a
speech which could not be safely repeated anywhere on Southern soil in this enlightened year.
But while there were some differences of opinion on this subject even then, discussion was
allowed ; but as you see by the Kansas slave
code, which, as you know, is the Missouri slave
code, merely ferried across the river, it is a
felony to even express an opinion hostile to that

foul blot in the land of Washington and the Declaration of Independence.   [Sensation.]

In Kentucky—my State—in 1849, on a test vote, the mighty influence of Henry Clay and many other good men there could not get a symptom of expression in favor of gradual emancipation on a plain issue of marching toward the light of civilization with Ohio and Illinois ; but the State of Boone and Hardin and Henry Clay, with a *nigger* under each arm, took the black trail toward the deadly swamps of barbarism.   Is there—can there be —any doubt about this thing ? And is there any doubt that we must all lay aside our prejudices and march, shoulder to shoulder, in the great army of Freedom ? [Applause.]

Every Fourth of July our young orators all proclaim this to be " the land of the *free* and the home of the brave !"   Well, now, when you orators get that off next year, and, may be, this very year, how would you like some old grizzled farmer to get up in the grove and deny it ? [Laughter.]   How would you like that ? But suppose Kansas comes in as a slave State, and all the " border ruffians" have barbecues about it, and free-State men come trailing back to the dishonored North, like whipped dogs with their tails between their legs, it is—ain't it ?—evident that this is no more the " land of the free ;" and if we let it go so, we won't dare to say " home of the brave" out loud.   [Sensation and confusion.]

Abraham Lincoln

Can any man doubt that, even in spite of the people's will, slavery will triumph through violence, unless that will be made manifest and enforced ? Even Governor Reeder claimed at the outset that the contest in Kansas was to be fair, but he got his eyes open at last ; and I believe that, as a result of this moral and physical violence, Kansas will soon apply for admission as a slave State. And yet we can't mistake that the people don't want it so, and that it is a land which is free both by natural and political law. *No law is free law !* Such is the understanding of all Christendom. In the Somerset case, decided nearly a century ago, the great Lord Mansfield held that slavery was of such a nature that it must take its rise in *positive* (as distinguished from *natural*) law ; and that in no country or age could it be traced back to any other source. Will some one please tell me where is the *positive* law that establishes slavery in Kansas ? [A voice : " The *bogus* laws."] Aye, the *bogus* laws ! And, on the same principle, a gang of Missouri horse-thieves could come into Illinois and declare horse-stealing to be legal [Laughter], and it would be just as legal as slavery is in Kansas. But by express statute, in the land of Washington and Jefferson, we may soon be brought face to face with the discreditable fact of showing to the world by our acts that we prefer slavery to freedom—darkness to light ! [Sensation]

It is, I believe, a principle in law that when

one party to a contract violates it so grossly as to chiefly destroy the object for which it is made, the other party may rescind it. I will ask Browning if that ain't good law. [Voices : " Yes !"] Well, now if that be right, I go for rescinding the whole, entire Missouri Compromise and thus turning Missouri into a free State ; and I should like to know the difference —should like for any one to point out the difference—between *our* making a free State of Missouri and *their* making a slave State of Kansas. [Great applause.] There ain't one bit of difference, except that our way would be a great mercy to humanity. But I have never said— and the Whig party has never said—and those who oppose the Nebraska bill do not as a body say, that they have any intention of interfering with slavery in the slave States. Our platform says just the contrary. We allow slavery to exist in the slave States—not because slavery is right or good, but from the necessities of our Union. We grant a fugitive slave law because it is so " nominated in the bond ;" because our fathers so stipulated—had to—and we are bound to carry out this agreement. But they did not agree to introduce slavery in regions where it did not previously exist. On the contrary, they said by their example and teachings that they did not deem it expedient—did not consider it right—to do so ; and it is wise and right to do just as they did about it [Voices : " Good !"], and that is what we propose—not to interfere with slavery where it exists (we have never tried to do it), and to give them a reasonable and efficient fugitive slave law. [A voice : " No !"] I say YES ! [Applause.] It was part of the bargain, and I'm for living up to it ; but I go no further ; I'm not bound to do more, and I won't agree any further. [Great applause.]

We, here in Illinois, should feel especially proud of the provision of the Missouri Compromise excluding slavery from what is now Kansas ; for an Illinois man, Jesse B. Thomas, was its father. Henry Clay, who is credited with the authorship of the Compromise in general terms, did not even vote for that provision, but only advocated the ultimate admission by a second compromise ; and Thomas was, beyond all controversy, the real author of the " slavery restriction" branch of the Compromise. To show the generosity of the Northern members toward the Southern side ; on a test vote to exclude slavery from Missouri, ninety voted not to exclude, and eighty-seven to exclude, every vote from the slave States being ranged with the former and fourteen votes from the free States, of whom seven were from New England alone ; while on a vote to exclude slavery from what is now Kansas, the vote was one hundred and thirty-four *for* to forty-two *against*. The scheme, as a whole, was, of course, a Southern triumph. It is idle to contend otherwise, as is now being done by the Nebraskaites ; it was so shown by the votes and quite as emphatically by the expressions of representative men. Mr. Lowndes of South Carolina was never known to commit a political mistake ; his was the great judgment of that section ; and he declared that this measure " would restore tranquillity to the country—a result demanded by every consideration of discretion, of moderation, of wisdom, and of virtue." When the measure came before President Monroe for his approval, he put to each member of his cabinet this question : " Has Congress the constitutional power to prohibit slavery in a territory?" And John C. Calhoun and William H. Crawford from the South, equally with John Quincy Adams, Benjamin Rush, and Smith Thompson from the North, alike answered, " *Yes !*" without qualification or equivocation ; and this measure, of so great consequence to the South, was passed ; and Missouri was, by means of it, finally enabled to knock at the door of the Republic for an open passage to its brood of slaves. And, in spite of this, Freedom's share is about to be taken by violence—by the force of misrepresentative votes, not called for by the popular will. What name can I, in common decency, give to this wicked transaction ? [Sensation.]

But even then the contest was not over ; for when the Missouri constitution came before Congress for its approval, it forbade any free negro or mulatto from entering the State. In short, our Illinois "black laws" were hidden away in their constitution [Laughter], and the controversy was thus revived. Then it was that Mr. Clay's talents shone out conspicuously, and the controversy that shook the Union to its foundation was finally settled to the satisfaction of the conservative parties' on both sides of the line, though not to the extremists on either, and Missouri was admitted by the small majority of six in the lower House. How great a majority, do you think, would have been given had Kansas also been secured for slavery? [A voice: "A majority the other way."] "A majority the other way," is answered. Do you think it would have been safe for a Northern man to have confronted his constituents after having voted to consign both Missouri and Kansas to hopeless slavery? And yet this man Douglas, who misrepresents his constituents and who has exerted his highest talents in that direction, will be carried in triumph through the State and hailed with honor while applauding that act. [Three groans for "*Dug!*"] And this shows whither we are tending. This thing of slavery is more powerful than its supporters— even than the high priests that minister at its altar. It debauches even our greatest men. It gathers strength, like a rolling snow-ball, by its own infamy. Monstrous crimes are committed in its name by persons collectively which they would not dare to commit as individuals. Its aggressions and encroachments almost surpass

"Lincoln's Lost Speech"

belief. In a despotism, one might not wonder
to see slavery advance steadily and remorse-
lessly into new dominions ; but is it not wonderful, is it not even alarming, to see its steady
advance in a land dedicated to the proposition
that "all men are created equal"? [Sensa-
tion.]

It yields nothing itself ; it keeps all it has,
and gets all it can besides. It really came dangerously near securing Illinois in 1824 ; it did
get Missouri in 1821. The first proposition was
to admit what is now Arkansas *and* Missouri as
one slave State. But the territory was divided,
and Arkansas came in, without serious question, as a slave State ; and afterward Missouri,
not as a sort of equality, *free*, but also as a
slave State. Then we had Florida and Texas ;
and now Kansas is about to be forced into the
dismal procession. [Sensation.] And so it is
wherever you look. We have not forgotten—
it is but six years since—how dangerously near
California came to being a slave State. Texas
is a slave State, and four other slave States may
be carved from its vast domain. · And yet, in
the year 1829, slavery was abolished throughout
that vast region by a royal decree of the then
sovereign of Mexico. Will you please tell me
by what *right* slavery exists in Texas to-day?
By the same right as, and no higher or greater
than, slavery is seeking dominion in Kansas :
by political force—peaceful, if that will suffice ;
by the torch (as in Kansas) and the bludgeon

155

Abraham Lincoln

(as in the Senate chamber), if required. And so history repeats itself ; and even as slavery has kept its course by craft, intimidation, and violence in the past, so it will persist, in my judgment, until met and dominated by the will of a people bent on its restriction.

We have, this very afternoon, heard bitter denunciations of Brooks in Washington, and Titus, Stringfellow, Atchison, Jones, and Shannon in Kansas—the battle-ground of slavery. I certainly am not going to advocate or shield them ; but they and their acts are but the necessary outcome of the Nebraska law. We should reserve our highest censure for the authors of the mischief, and not for the catspaws which they use. I believe it was Shakespeare who said, " Where the offense lies, there let the axe fall ;" and, in my opinion, this man Douglas and the Northern men in Congress who advocate " Nebraska" are more guilty than a thousand Joneses and Stringfellows, with all their murderous practices, can be. [Applause.]

We have made a good beginning here to-day. As our Methodist friends would say, " I feel it is good to be here." While extremists may find some fault with the moderation of our platform, they should recollect that " the battle is not always to the strong, nor the race to the swift." In grave emergencies, moderation is generally safer than radicalism ; and as this struggle is likely to be long and earnest, we must not, by our action, repel any who are in sympathy with us in the main, but rather win all that we can to our standard.. We must not belittle nor overlook the facts of our condition —that we are new and comparatively weak, while our enemies are entrenched and relatively strong. They have the administration and the political power ; and, right or wrong, at present they have the numbers. Our friends who urge an appeal to arms with so much force and elo- quence, should recollect that the government is arrayed against us, and that the numbers are now arrayed against us as well ; or, to state it nearer to the truth, they are not yet expressly and affirmatively for us ; and we should repel friends rather than gain them by anything savoring of revolutionary methods. As it now stands, we must appeal to the sober sense and patriotism of the people. We will make con- verts day by day ; we will grow strong by calm- ness and moderation ; we will grow strong by the violence and injustice of our adversaries. And, unless truth be a mockery and justice a hollow lie, we will be in the majority after a while, and then the revolution which we will accomplish will be none the less radical from being the result of pacific measures. The bat- tle of freedom is to be fought out on principle. Slavery is a violation of the eternal right. We have temporized with it from the necessities of our condition ; but *as sure as God reigns and school children read*, THAT BLACK FOUL LIE CAN NEVER BE CONSECRATED INTO GOD'S HALLOWED

TRUTH ! [Immense applause lasting some time.] One of our greatest difficulties is, that men who *know* that slavery is a detestable crime and ruinous to the nation, are compelled, by our peculiar condition and other circumstances, to advocate it concretely, though damning it in the raw. Henry Clay was a brilliant example of this tendency ; others of our purest statesmen are compelled to do so ; and thus slavery secures actual support from those who detest it at heart. Yet Henry Clay perfected and forced through the Compromise which secured to slavery a great State as well as a political advantage. Not that he hated slavery less, but that he loved the whole Union more. As long as slavery profited by his great Compromise, the hosts of pro-slavery could not sufficiently cover him with praise ; but now that this Compromise stands in their way—

" . . . they never mention him,
His name is never heard :
Their lips are now forbid to speak
That once familiar word."

They have slaughtered one of his most cherished measures, and his ghost would arise to rebuke them. [Great applause.]

Now, let us harmonize, my friends, and appeal to the moderation and patriotism of the people : to the sober second thought ; to the awakened public conscience. The repeal of the sacred Missouri Compromise has installed the weapons of violence : the bludgeon, the in-

cendiary torch, the death-dealing rifle, the
bristling cannon—the weapons of kingcraft, of
the inquisition, of ignorance, of barbarism, of
oppression. We see its fruits in the dying bed
of the heroic Sumner ; in the ruins of the " Free
State" hotel ; in the smoking embers of the
Herald of Freedom ; in the free-State Governor of Kansas chained to a stake on freedom's
soil like a horse-thief, for the crime of freedom.
[Applause.] We see it in Christian statesmen,
and Christian newspapers, and Christian pulpits, applauding *the cowardly act of a low
bully*, WHO CRAWLED UPON HIS VICTIM BEHIND
HIS BACK AND DEALT THE DEADLY BLOW. [Sen-
sation and applause.] We note our political
demoralization in the catch-words that are coming into such common use ; on the one hand,
" freedom-shriekers," and sometimes " free-
dom-screechers" [Laughter] ; and, on the other
hand, " border ruffians," and that fully de-
served. And the significance of catch-words
cannot pass unheeded, for they constitute a
sign of the times. Everything in this world
" jibes" in with everything else, and all the
fruits of this Nebraska bill are like the poisoned
source from which they come. I will not say
that we may not sooner or later be compelled
to meet force by force ; but the time has not
yet come, and if we are true to ourselves, may
never come. Do not mistake that the ballot is
stronger than the bullet. Therefore let the
legions of slavery use bullets ; but let us wait

patiently till November, and fire ballots at them in return ; and by that peaceful policy, I believe we shall ultimately win. [Applause.]

It was by that policy that here in Illinois the early fathers fought the good fight and gained the victory. In 1824 the free men of our State, led by Governor Coles (who was a native of Maryland and President Madison's private secretary), determined that those beautiful groves should never reëcho the dirge of one who has no title to himself. By their resolute determination, the winds that sweep across our broad prairies shall never cool the parched brow, nor shall the unfettered streams that bring joy and gladness to our free soil water the tired feet, of a *slave ;* but so long as those heavenly breezes and sparkling streams bless the land, or the groves and their fragrance or their memory remain, the humanity to which they minister SHALL BE FOREVER FREE ! [Great applause.] Palmer, Yates, Williams, Browning, and some more in this convention came from Kentucky to Illinois (instead of going to Missouri), not only to better their conditions, but also to get away from slavery. They have said so to me, and it is understood among us Kentuckians that we don't like it one bit. Now, can we, mindful of the blessings of liberty which the early men of Illinois left to us, refuse a like privilege to the free men who seek to plant Freedom's banner on our Western outposts? [" No ! No !"] Should we not stand by our

"Lincoln's Lost Speech"

neighbors who seek to better their conditions
in Kansas and Nebraska? [" Yes! Yes!"]
Can we as Christian men, and strong and free
ourselves, wield the sledge or hold the iron
which is to manacle anew an already oppressed
race? [" No! No!"] "Woe unto them," it
is written, " that decree unrighteous decrees
and that write grievousness which they have
prescribed." Can we afford to sin any more
deeply against human liberty? [" No! No!"]

One great trouble in the matter is, that
slavery is an insidious and crafty power, and
gains equally by open violence of the brutal as
well as by sly management of the peaceful.
Even after the ordinance of 1787, the settlers in
Indiana and Illinois (it was all one government
then) tried to get Congress to allow slavery
temporarily, and petitions to that end were sent
from Kaskaskia, and General Harrison, the
Governor, urged it from Vincennes, the capital. If that had succeeded, good-by to liberty
here. But John Randolph of Virginia made a
vigorous report against it ; and although they
persevered so well as to get three favorable re-
ports for it, yet the United States Senate, with
the aid of some slave States, finally *squelched*
it for good. [Applause.] And that is why
this hall is to-day a temple for free men instead
of a negro livery stable. [Great applause and
laughter.] Once let slavery get planted in a
locality, by ever so weak or doubtful a title, and
in ever so small numbers, and it is like the Can-

ada thistle or Bermuda grass—you can't root it out. You yourself may detest slavery; but your neighbor has five or six slaves, and he is an excellent neighbor, or your son has married his daughter, and they beg you to help save their property, and you vote against your interest and principles to accommodate a neighbor, hoping that your vote will be on the losing side. And others do the same; and in those ways slavery gets a sure foothold. And when that is done the whole mighty Union—the force of the nation—is committed to its support. And that very process is working in Kansas to-day. And you must recollect that the slave property is worth a billion of dollars ($1,000,000,000); while free-State men must work for sentiment alone. Then there are "blue lodges"—as they call them—everywhere doing their secret and deadly work.

It is a very strange thing, and not solvable by any moral law that I know of, that if a man loses his horse, the whole country will turn out to help hang the thief; but if a man but a shade or two darker than I am is himself stolen, the same crowd will hang one who aids in restoring him to liberty. Such are the inconsistencies of slavery, where a horse is more sacred than a man; and the essence of *squatter* or popular sovereignty—I don't care how you call it—is that if one man chooses to make a slave of another, no third man shall be allowed to object. And if you can do this in free Kansas,

" Lincoln's Lost Speech "

and it is allowed to stand, the next thing you
will see is ship loads of negroes from Africa at
the wharf at Charleston ; for one thing is as
truly lawful as the other ; and these are the
bastard notions we have got to stamp out, else
they will stamp us out. [Sensation and applause.]

Two years ago, at Springfield, Judge Douglas
avowed that Illinois came into the Union as a
slave State, and that slavery was weeded out
by the operation of his great, patent, ever-
lasting principle of " popular sovereignty."
[Laughter.] Well, now, that argument must
be answered, for it has a little grain of truth at
the bottom. I do not mean that it is true in
essence, as he would have us believe. It could
not be essentially true if the ordinance of '87
was valid. But, in point of fact, there were
some degraded beings called slaves in Kaskaskia and the other French settlements when our
first State constitution was adopted ; that is a
fact, and I don't deny it. Slaves were brought
here as early as 1720, and were kept here in
spite of the ordinance of 1787 against it. But
slavery did not thrive here. On the contrary,
under the influence of the ordinance, the number *decreased* fifty-one from 1810 to 1820 ; while
under the influence of *squatter* sovereignty,
right across the river in Missouri, they *increased*
seven thousand two hundred and eleven in the
same time ; and slavery finally faded out in
Illinois, under the influence of the law of free-

dom, while it grew stronger and stronger in Missouri, under the law or practice of "popular sovereignty." In point of fact there were but one hundred and seventeen slaves in Illinois one year after its admission, or one to every four hundred and seventy of its population ; or, to state it in another way, if Illinois was a slave State in 1820, so were New York and New Jersey much greater slave States from having had greater numbers, slavery having been established there in very early times. But there is this vital difference between all these States and the judge's Kansas experiment : that they sought to disestablish slavery which had been already established, while the judge seeks, so far as he can, to disestablish freedom, which had been established there by the Missouri Compromise. [Voices : " Good !"]

The Union is undergoing a fearful strain ; but it is a stout old ship, and has weathered many a hard blow, and " the stars , in their courses," aye, an invisible power, greater than the puny efforts of men, will fight for us. But we ourselves must not decline the burden of responsibility, nor take counsel of unworthy passions. Whatever duty urges us to do or to omit, must be done or omitted ; and the recklessness with which our adversaries break the laws, or counsel their violation, should afford no example for us. Therefore, let us revere the Declaration of Independence ; let us continue to obey the Constitution and the laws ;

.et us keep step to the music of the Union. Let
is draw a cordon, so to speak, around the slave
States, and the hateful institution, like a reptile
poisoning itself, will perish by its own infamy.
[Applause.]

But we cannot be free men if this is, by our
national choice, to be a land of slavery. Those
who deny freedom to others, deserve it not for
themselves ; and, under the rule of a just God,
cannot long retain it. [Loud applause.]

Did you ever, my friends, seriously reflect
upon the speed with which we are tending
downward ? Within the memory of men now
present the leading statesmen of Virginia could
make genuine, red-hot abolitionist speeches in
old Virginia ; and, as I have said, now even in
" free Kansas" it is a crime to declare that it is
" free Kansas." The very sentiments that I
and others have just uttered would entitle us,
and each of us, to the ignominy and seclusion
of a dungeon ; and yet I suppose that, like
Paul, we were " free born." But if this thing
is allowed to continue, it will be but one step
further to impress the same rule in Illinois.
[Sensation.]

The conclusion of all is, that we must restore
the Missouri Compromise. We must highly resolve that *Kansas must be free!* [Great applause.] We must reinstate the birthday promise of the Republic ; we must reaffirm the Declaration of Independence ; we must make good
in essence as well as in form Madison's avowal

that "the word *slave* ought not to appear in the Constitution ;" and we must even go further, and decree that only local law, and not that time-honored instrument, shall shelter a slave-holder. We must make this a land of liberty in fact, as it is in name. But in seeking to attain these results—so indispensable if the liberty which is our pride and boast shall endure—we will be loyal to the Constitution and to the "flag of our Union," and no matter what our grievance—even though Kansas shall come in as a slave State ; and no matter what theirs—even if we shall restore the Compromise —WE WILL SAY TO THE SOUTHERN DISUNIONISTS, WE WON'T GO OUT OF THE UNION, AND YOU SHAN'T ! ! ! [This was the climax ; the audience rose to its feet *en masse*, applauded, stamped, waved handkerchiefs, threw hats in the air, and ran riot for several minutes. The arch-enchanter who wrought this transformation looked, meanwhile, like the personification of political justice.]

But let us, meanwhile, appeal to the sense and patriotism of the people, and not to their prejudices ; let us spread the floods of enthusiasm here aroused all over these vast prairies, so suggestive of freedom. Let us commence by electing the gallant soldier Governor (Colonel) Bissell who stood for the honor of our State alike on the plains and amidst the chaparral of Mexico and on the floor of Congress, while he defied the Southern Hotspur ; and

that will have a greater moral effect than all
the border ruffians can accomplish in all their
raids on Kansas.   There is both a power and a
magic in popular opinion.   To that let us now
appeal ; and while, in all probability, no resort
to force will be needed, our moderation and
forbearance will stand us in good stead when,
if ever, WE MUST MAKE AN APPEAL TO BATTLE AND
TO THE GOD OF HOSTS ! !   [Immense applause
and a rush for the orator.]

www.ingramcontent.com/pod-product-compliance
Lightning Source LLC
Chambersburg PA
CBHW031112020726
47495CB00007B/2160